SKINNED

A gripping crime thriller full of twists

EMMY ELLIS

Detective Tracy Collier Book 3

Originally published as
All Her Fears

JOFFE BOOKS

Revised edition 2024
Joffe Books, London
www.joffebooks.com

First published in Great Britain in 2018
as *All Her Fears*

This paperback edition was first published
in Great Britain in 2024

Cover art by Dee Dee Books Covers

ISBN: 978-1-83526-353-2

PROLOGUE

Last Week

She's about to find out he's not who she thought he was.

He glares at her. "Stay there. Don't move. If you do, I'll kill you."

She laughs at him, her head thrown back against the wall, her alcohol-addled brain probably refusing to accept what he'd said. It isn't funny. He wasn't being funny.

She'll understand that soon.

Seems she doesn't have a clue where they are, as though she's forgotten the journey here, where she'd tottered on her spindly legs through the dark backstreets, then along the country road for around five miles. She'd skidded down a verge at one point, squealing, and he'd hauled her back onto the roadside, where the urge to hurt her had been almost too strong to ignore.

Why hadn't she questioned their destination? It's not every man who takes a woman to a disused part of a building, is it, where he'll keep her there until she's done what he wants.

Her hair doesn't look so nice now they're in brighter light. It's stringy from sweat where she'd got all hot and bothered walking here.

The humidity lately is a killer.

"You're so funny," she says, eyeing him as though she doesn't find him funny at all.

"I'm being serious. Don't move."

She blinks a few times, and it seems something's dawning in her mind, the realisation she's not as safe as she thought. That she isn't going to have sex and make it home tonight.

No, this one can stay.

Here.

Until he needs her services.

Her head tilts to one side, and her eyes cloud over with what might be fear — or is that shutters coming down, where this situation feels familiar and memories have come flooding back?

"What . . . what's going on?" She frowns, her eyebrows dipping low.

"You'll see soon enough. Now be quiet. You're getting on my nerves."

He steps forward, shoves a rag in her mouth, then uses rope to secure her wrists and ankles. Perhaps she thinks this is the way he likes it. Rough.

Perhaps she thinks she can leave once they've done the business.

Except there won't be any business.

Not the kind she's expecting anyway.

CHAPTER ONE

Her laughter reminds me of a burbling stream, and I grit my teeth.

"Come on now, Mrs Roberts, I need to get you into bed before nine. You know the rules." I smile and nod, hands on hips, hoping I fare better at getting her to obey than the other nurse had last night.

This old woman here, wanting to talk and laugh about the good old days, isn't helping my schedule. If we can get everyone tucked in by eight instead of the usual nine, I'll call that a win. There's a good film on we all want to watch. The other nurses are having a cup of tea — the staff deserve a peaceful night after the hassle from Mrs Roberts yesterday and today. It seems the old woman doesn't want to do as she's told anymore. She's already frazzled the nerves of the daytime staff and is intent on frazzling mine now, too.

"I don't want to go to bed," Mrs Roberts says. "It's too early. I have to wait until you've set the alarm."

"It isn't early. It's just right. And we'll lock up soon." I smile. "In you get."

She stands beside her bed, her expression one of worry. "Please don't make me. He said he'll come for me if I go to sleep."

"Pardon me?" I lift my eyebrows and give her my best glare. *Who is 'he'?*

"Plus, my son said—"

"I'm not interested in what your son has to say. He put you in here and knows the rules."

"But it isn't nine yet," she whines, twisting a strand of hair around a finger in agitation.

"No, but tonight is different."

"Why?"

I grit my teeth again. It hurts. Why am I getting angry with her? I'm not usually so wound up. It's like I'm a different person from time to time. "It's not for you to ask why. Now get into bed."

"No." She folds her arms over her rounded belly and stamps one foot. "I have rights. I should feel safe here, and I don't."

I sigh, leave the room, and head for the next old fart's. That woman back there . . . well, I'll deal with her later. Annoyed at being challenged, I thump open Mrs Klark's door, and she all but jumps a foot off her flower-patterned chair. Slim to the point of being a skeleton covered in skin, Mrs Klark gawps at me from behind thick-lens glasses, her eyes appearing golf-ball sized. Her scalp shines through her sparse, wispy white hair, and I hold back a bark that she should be wearing her bloody hat like she's been told to.

Calm down. Be Chrissy, the real Chrissy.

"Come along, Mrs Klark. Bedtime is earlier tonight."

She nods and pushes herself up using the armrests. I'm surprised her wrists don't snap.

Mrs Klark is already in her long, light-blue nightdress, and she shuffles over to her bed, the scrape of her slippers over the carpet bringing on a red mist. It threatens to cloud my judgement, so I take a deep breath while she pops her glasses on the sideboard then settles under the quilt, the edge right up to her neck.

"You're a good girl, Mrs Klark, aren't you?"

I switch out the light then leave. Sorting out ten other ancient dears proves just as easy as my time with Klark, and

I release some tension, rolling my shoulders and reminding myself that if Mrs Roberts finally does as she's told, the nurses will have a nice, quiet night.

I enter her room, and she stares at me from her leather recliner, mouth trembling. A programme about lions plays on her small TV, the animals roaring then chasing after unsuspecting prey.

"Right, it's closer to the usual bedtime now, Mrs Roberts, so come along."

She lifts her chin. "My programme hasn't finished. I watch this every week."

"Look, you need your medicine as well, and I haven't got time for you to mess me about."

"Please don't let him hurt me," she says.

Who the hell is she gabbling on about?

Once again, I leave her. I don't know what to do to make her follow the rules.

* * *

He strides to the medicine laid out for this evening in the locked storeroom. With two syringes selected, he sorts out what will shut her up plus her usual drugs, then returns just as the closing credits for her infernal programme flows up the screen.

"Get to bed," he says to that old Roberts bitch who has caused so much trouble.

"Yes . . . okay . . ."

Onto the mattress she gets, and he jabs the needle into her arm, depressing the plunger until all the liquid has gone in. She'll be out in no time. Then he administers the medication she's supposed to have, and she opens her mouth to speak, but no words come out.

"This is what happens when you do things that ruins families," he says then leaves the room, disposing of one syringe in the proper manner and slipping the other in his pocket.

He leaves Blooming Age and, at the nearest supermarket, picks up a tray of Krispy Kreme assorted doughnuts, pays for them, then, once outside, dumps the second syringe in the bin beside the door.

He hopes, when he gets back, the carers are still sitting in the staff room, waiting for the film to start.

It won't do to have one of them check the olds and find Mrs Roberts dead yet.

No, it won't do at all.

CHAPTER TWO

The phone rang on her desk, and Tracy reluctantly answered it. "DI Collier."

"Vic Atkins, boss."

Tracy closed her eyes momentarily — she didn't need a new job on her hands. Not today. The serious crimes squad she ran had recently wrapped up a case regarding three brothers — same father, different mothers. With the paperwork finally completed, her team now worked on other, smaller crimes while they waited for the next biggie to turn up. They needed a bit more of a breather, the calm before another almighty storm, but if Vic from the front desk was on the blower, that dream of having time between was looking more like a sodding nightmare.

"Shit, Vic. Bad news, is it?"

"You could say that. Happy Monday to you. A body's been found."

"You're kidding me . . ." Adrenaline punched into her system, and she swallowed bile that had shot up.

"No, boss. Not something I find amusing, death."

"Me neither — and you know what I meant."

"I did. Just fancied being facetious."

"Well . . . don't." She sighed, raking a hand through her ginger hair. It'd need a dye-job soon, what with the amount of grey she'd spotted this morning in the bathroom mirror, and her only young. Ish. "Come on then. What have you got?"

"Odd one. An old lady in her nightie."

"What?" She scratched her head. "And this is coming to me because . . . ?"

"She didn't just wander out of her house and fall down dead, boss. She had her throat slit."

"Fuck me sideways," she muttered. "All right. Address of the crime scene, please. And you'll get hold of Gilbert for me, won't you?" A bright spot to the day. Gilbert, the pathologist, would have her laughing in no time. She needed a mood lightener after the past few months worrying her arse off about whether her deranged sister, Lisa, would show her spiteful face again.

Something I don't need either.

Vic gave the address, and Tracy jotted it down.

"Yep, I'll get hold of Gilbert for you now, boss."

"All right. I'm on my way."

She replaced the receiver in the cradle, sighing again. At this rate, the town was going to end up like one of those weird ones in books and on TV, where everyone got killed once a month and the residents still remained, not thinking anything of living in place where people kept getting bumped off.

Rising, she slung her jacket on and made her way to the incident room, which also served as a permanent, large office where her team worked. She stood in front of the three whiteboards and faced the gang.

Damon, her partner at work and in life, raised his eyebrows. Yes, he knew what was coming, could probably tell just from a micro-expression on her face. Nada glanced up from her monitor and tilted her head. Tracy gave her a slight nod.

"Right, team. Talk about not getting a moment to breathe. We have a new murder to deal with."

Lara and Erica snapped their heads up, while Tim and Alastair groaned.

"Sorry, thought we'd be able to work the smaller cases some more, get them closed and off our backs, but fate has other ideas. Bollocks, I know, but it's what we're here for, so we need to get to it." Tracy pinched her chin. "Not much to go on — an old lady, throat slit."

Someone hissed.

"Indeed. Nasty." Tracy glanced at Damon. "I'll be off with Damon. You guys continue what you've been doing. When I know the victim's name, Nada, I'll call in so you can all do that needs to be done." She pointed to the printouts she'd attached to one of the boards with Blu Tack. "This is a chance for us to put my new game plan into action." She tapped the A4 paper. "You all have specific jobs to be getting on with once we know who the victim is. Family members, friends, bank records, work colleagues, social media accounts, CCTV, phone use. You're on it like flies on shit, okay? This saves me actioning every little thing — and it means I trust you to get on with it." She pressed a hand to the space beneath the A4. "You tick off on the sheet when you've done your tasks and write your information down here. Got it?"

A flurry of *yes, boss*, then, "We've got it," from Nada. "I made sure everyone recited what they had to do when a new case comes up — every day for the past fortnight we've been getting it into our heads."

Tracy smiled at Nada — the woman was a marvel. "You're a godsend. Thank you. Right, we're off. I'll ring in as soon as I have anything." She scribbled the address where she'd be on the first board and tapped it so the team got the gist. Then she walked to the door and paused. "Oh, Nada, while we're out, get on to missing persons and see if any elderly women have been reported as AWOL. If Chief Winter asks where me and Damon are, let him know, will you? Thanks."

She took the three flights of stairs at a clip, the downward momentum fuelling the rush careening through her at having a grisly case so soon after the last. Footsteps scuffed and squeaked above, signalling Damon followed.

In the car park, she took a deep breath of exhaust-fume air and headed to her car. She'd switched it out to a different model so her damn sister wouldn't know which one she drove now. Then again, Tracy's bright hair would be a dead giveaway should Lisa be hanging around the station, watching. Maybe it was time to take a leaf from Lisa's demented book and opt for a different colour completely. Lisa's had been dyed black in her attempt to disguise herself, but Tracy and Damon had recognised her recently when she'd turned up, unbidden and definitely unwanted.

Bloody woman had better not show her face again.

In the car, Tracy waited for Damon to catch up. He flung himself into the passenger seat, panting, his breathing not too hot these days since Lisa had stabbed him. Not that Damon knew Lisa was Tracy's sister. He thought she was just some woman who'd lived with Tracy's dad.

What a fucked-up situation.

"Ready?" she asked.

"This'll be tough because she's old." Damon plugged in his seat belt.

"Yep, but they're all tough, no matter their age." She prodded the address into the satnav then gunned the engine and headed for the scene, the GPS's voice no longer Australian from when Damon had switched it over as a joke.

They didn't speak, Tracy lost inside her head, thinking of where Lisa might be. Damon left her alone to do it. He knew better than to interrupt her when she zoned out. The crime scene was five hundred yards ahead, according to the patient-sounding but irritating satnav lady, a field by the look of it, a police car and a PC standing on the verge, although she couldn't work out who it was yet. She still had a few coppers she hadn't met, her being newish to the station.

Tracy parked, and she and Damon got out. Ah, PC Newson, it was, and he smiled, holding out the crime scene log for them to sign, a far cry from the first time she'd met him when he'd been suspicious of who she was, a new DI on the block.

"Morning," she said, scribbling her name and the time on the tablet using the red plastic pen attached to it by string. "PC York with the body?"

Newson nodded while Damon signed the log.

"Let's hope she's taken better precautions this time." Tracy dipped her hand into a cardboard box at Newson's feet and helped herself to white protective clothing and gloves. She put them on, as did Damon. This would be the first time Tracy had seen Simone York since she'd had a word with her sergeant about being careful at scenes. At the last one, Simone hadn't been too bothered about where she was putting her size fives, scrunching through the leaves as though it didn't matter, and it had got Tracy's goat. "Where are we going?" she asked Newson.

"Just behind the hedge, ma'am. Um, boss."

"Right. Thank you." She suspected York would have heard what she'd said about her, but she didn't give much of a shit.

Tracy shrugged and went to push through a gap in the hedge but stopped. Was it the one the killer had made when either bringing the old lady out here to kill her or dumping her body?

"Um, can you move along a bit, Newson, please?"

He did as he'd been told.

"It's just that the killer might have been right here, and we're fucking up the scene."

"Um, I doubt it, boss." Newson pointed along the road ahead. "There's a path up there. Blood on it. I put scene tape up. The path cuts across the field. There's a wire fence either side of it and a gate in the middle a few metres in. Apparently leads to the farmer's house — that's who found her."

Tracy looked that way. A piece of tape fluttered on the bush. "Thank you. Did you speak to the farmer already, or did someone else do that?"

"It was me." He grimaced. "Poor bloke was about to let his cows out to graze and saw the woman's nightie — said it stood out because it's white."

"Take a statement, did you? His address?"

"Yes, boss. If you turn around, you can see the farmhouse from here. There's an access road just past the path."

"Righty ho. So, I'll just go through the hedge then. Did York make the gap?"

"No. She stayed there after we'd walked over the field from the farmhouse. That's where we went first."

"Okay. Stick up a bit of tape here. It's bothering me there's a gap. Someone's obviously made it. Or maybe it's one of the cows. We'll take the path, seeing as we're suited and booted."

She led the way, and Damon jogged to her side. They ducked beneath the tape and walked along the pale-coloured path, blood spatter dotted in various places.

They entered the left side of the field via the gate and tromped over towards the body and PC York, who straightened upon their approach and gave a nervous smile.

"Glad to see you've got booties on this time, York," Tracy said.

"Thought I'd better, ma'am."

The low roar of traffic interrupted them, and Tracy peered through the leaves of the hedge. Gilbert had arrived along with SOCO. "You can go and stand with Newson now." She smiled at York.

While they waited for Gilbert, Damon said, "I don't want to look at her. The old lady." He jerked his head in the direction of the body to their left, lying against the base of the hedge.

"No, can't say I fancy it much either." Tracy swallowed the lump in her throat. This was someone's gran, their mum, sister, aunt. What the hell the world was coming to she didn't know. "Ah, here's Gilbert now."

He walked down the path towards the gate.

"Here's hoping he's on top form," she said. "I could do with cheering up."

Damon shook his head. "I'll just wait over here. I'm not in the mood for his dark jokes."

It was a good job Tracy was then, wasn't it?

CHAPTER THREE

"Good morning to you, Tracy, Damon." Gilbert beamed and pulled a plastic sheet out of his black case and held it. "We'll get the photos done of her in situ, then I can pop her on this." He held the folded sheet up. "Ah, here's our guy now."

Tracy, Damon, and Gilbert moved away so the photographer could do his job.

"I heard from Kane," Gilbert said.

Tracy's hackles went up. DI Kane Barnett wasn't a name she wanted to hear right now. She was still angry with him for being a prick when she'd first turned up to take on the squad job. "That's nice for you."

Gilbert laughed. "Don't you want to know what he's up to?"

"Not really, but I suppose you're going to tell me anyway."

"He's tracking Charlotte Rothers down on Cornwall's police time now he's working for them." Gilbert nodded knowingly.

"That isn't news." Tracy sniffed. "I'm surprised you didn't hear sooner. He must have fallen for her hard." Tracy hoped Charlotte's life wouldn't be buggered up with Kane arriving in her new place of residence. She'd probably gone down south to get away from what had happened — she didn't need an ex-lover chasing after her. The woman had suffered domestic violence and had been terrorised in a neighbour's man cave or whatever the hell it was.

"All done," the photographer said. "I'm off over to the path. I'll be back once you've moved her to take more shots."

Tracy glanced that way. Mini numbered cones had already been placed where the blood was by a SOCO. She returned her attention to Gilbert, who'd crouched beside the body. Damon sighed and bowed his head.

Tracy took a deep breath and forced herself to look at the old woman properly. Her back faced them, curved — the foetal position seemed posed, her limbs too precisely placed for her to have just been dropped like that. Or maybe she'd curled up prior to being murdered — or during the kill.

Gilbert rose and snapped out the sheet then spread it on the grass. He put her on top — how he managed to do that by himself was anyone's guess. "She's in rigor, so she's pretty fresh."

Tracy winced at his candour and studied the body. She turned away when he lifted the nightie — the woman deserved respect even in death.

"You can look back now," Gilbert said. "Throat slit, left to right, so a right-handed person if killing from behind, left-handed if it was done from the front. I'd say it was from behind."

"How so?" Tracy asked.

"The depth of the cut. From behind, there's a deeper slice because the victim is leaning against you. From the front, you risk them falling backwards as you slash — less stability, unless they're on a bed or have something behind them."

"I see." Tracy turned to check Damon was okay. His face had paled, but he'd managed to hold on to his breakfast.

"She's in the seventy to eighty mark," Gilbert went on. "Or an old-looking sixty-something. No ID. Wouldn't have thought so anyway, considering how she's dressed. So what are you looking at, do you think?"

"Apart from an old dear with a second smile?" She sighed. "I don't know. Home invasion gone wrong? She's in bed, and someone breaks in, she makes a fuss, he kills her? I can't think what else it would be. If she'd had clothes on instead of a nightie, that would be a different matter."

"I'd say she was dead before her throat was cut." Gilbert peered closely, his nose too near to the gaping wound for Tracy's liking.

"How the hell can you tell that?"

"There isn't enough blood — if she'd been killed while alive, it would have drenched her. With no heart working to pump the blood, there's less gush. Around fifteen minutes after death, the blood clots . . . you get the idea. And she didn't die in the foetal position. Posterior lividity. She was lying flat on her back."

"So she died, someone brought her here, then posed her."

"I'd say so, but they'd have had to do that within three to six hours of her death, otherwise rigor would prevent it."

"So the blood on the path?"

"Most likely isn't the victim's. What you see here on her nightdress is thick blood — cranberry sauce, if you will. That's nice with a bit of turkey, that is. Cranberry, not blood. It had already started clotting and moving to the back of her body, so the amount you see here . . . the killer most likely didn't get a scrap on them. The blood on the path is spatter, fresh, from a living person or someone just deceased. So unless there's another body floating around here somewhere . . ." Gilbert rose. "Well, she's not likely to be listening to *The Archers* anytime soon, is she?"

And there it was, Gilbert's beside-the-corpse joke.

"Took you long enough," Tracy said, allowing a grin to spread.

"I'm not on top form yet. Too early, not enough coffee." He winked and turned at the arrival of more SOCOs.

Tracy blew out a stream of breath. "I suppose we'd better crack on, see if we can find out who she is. I'm going to take a picture of her face." She snapped the shot, and while Gilbert prepared to take the body's temperature, she cropped the image down to remove sight of the gaping neck. Her phone vibrated as she hit save. She stared at the name on the screen: NADA. "Hmm. Might have a lead. Catch you soon."

She strode towards the middle of the field to answer. "Yep."

"Might have something for you, boss. A call came in earlier from a nursing home. Um . . . let me see now." The sound of paper being rustled filtered down the connection. "Yes, here. Blooming Age care facility. Reported a resident missing in the early hours of this morning. A Mrs Irene Roberts."

"Uniforms were sent out, I take it?"

"Yes, boss. Her son's there — he has an alibi apparently, according to the PC I spoke to. He was at some work do all night until three in the morning."

"Doesn't mean a thing if she was killed after that. Thanks, though. I'll nip there now and see what's what. Can you do the usual checks on Mrs Roberts and her family in the meantime? Thanks." Tracy cut the call and gestured to Damon.

They met up at the path and sidestepped the blood, markers, and SOCOs on hands and knees looking for other evidence.

Out on the verge, she said, "Old lady has gone missing from a nursing home. That was Nada on the phone."

"Shit." Damon shoved his hands into his pockets. "I heard what Gilbert said. If she was already dead, why bother slitting her throat?"

Tracy shrugged. "To make sure? Perverse pleasure? Who the fuck knows."

They removed their whites and stashed them in the boot. In the car, she entered the nursing home address, and they were off. She remained silent, thinking of the fact she'd never had a nan growing up, or a grandad come to that. Her parents had kept Tracy and Lisa to themselves — or she assumed they'd done that with Lisa. Her sister had been born before her, and once Tracy had come along, their father had hidden Lisa in the basement and told their mother she'd run away, then used his two daughters for his own perverted gain, along with Tracy's old chief, John.

Sick fucker.

Her father might be dead, but that didn't mean the memories had gone with him. They hadn't gone after she'd killed John either. She should have known those two men not being around anymore wouldn't change anything.

She took a left onto a long sweeping drive, a huge manor house at the end, probably used back in the day by some rich bastard or other. Now it was home to the elderly. Had the victim expected to see out her final days here? Maybe she actually had.

Tracy parked, and they exited, Tracy showing her ID to a PC standing at the top of the stone steps in front of the double, studded front doors. He nodded to her and Damon, then Tracy led the way inside. The wood-panelled foyer, more like a hotel's, had cream leather sofas against the left and right walls, low coffee tables in front of each, and a glossy mahogany reception desk ahead. People milled around, some staff in white nurse tops and navy trousers, the others God knew who.

Another PC stood talking to a tall, dark-haired man in his late forties, suit immaculate, black shoes shining. He bent his head then swiped his palms down his face — distressed?

Tracy approached the desk and flashed her card at the woman sitting behind it. She looked a lot like Angel, a different receptionist who'd sat behind a desk in another time, another place. A shiver rippled down Tracy's spine, and she plastered on a smile in the hopes it would shift the memories floating in her mind, back into the little box she kept inside her head where all bad things from the Past were kept.

She needed a new lock and key for it.

"I need to speak to someone about the missing person," she said.

"Oh, then you're better off talking to the head carer who was on duty last night. Chrissy Ordsall. She pulled a twelve-hour shift, so she's cranky."

"Thanks for the warning." Tracy turned to where the receptionist pointed.

A tall woman with a man's look about her stood with another lady, their heads bent, mouths moving. Ordsall appeared around forty. Her cheeks had a red stain to them, and she clenched her hands at her sides. Getting a dressing down, was she? It was understandable, what with a resident going missing on her shift. Not the best light to show yourself in, was it.

Not everyone can do all things, all the time, Tracy.

She acknowledged that truth. Before she'd created her job sheet at the station, she'd forgotten a few things in her time, like actioning tasks and even forgetting to do them herself. Although forgetting to check residents throughout the night, if that was what had happened, was a bit much to swallow.

You can say that when you've completely got your own shit together.

Hmm.

She headed for the women, showing them her ID. "Detective Inspector Tracy Collier, and this is my partner, DS Hanks. Is there somewhere we can talk in private?"

Ordsall visibly baulked, and Tracy hid a cringe, wondering if she had another Hilda Jones on her hands, a bear of a woman who'd got right on her tits on the last big case.

Don't do this to me, God.

Mind, God had allowed so many other things to happen to her, she didn't know why she was bothering to speak to Him again.

"The receiving room," the other lady said and held out her slender, pink-nailed hand. "I'm the manager, Mrs Zello. I wasn't here last night—"she gave Ordsall a filthy glance — "but Miss Ordsall was in charge. If you'd like to come this way . . ."

She strutted off in her six-inch scarlet heels and grey power suit, her brunette hair in the tightest chignon ever.

Tracy was surprised the woman's eyebrows hadn't stretched to her temples. Ordsall stomped behind her boss, and Tracy dared to look at Damon, who pressed his lips together and flushed as though holding back laughter.

"Don't," she said under her breath. "Another Jones I cannot deal with."

In the receiving room, much the same as the foyer but bigger and with more furniture, Ordsall stood by the floor-to-ceiling windows with a vast lawn beyond that stretched far more than Zello's eyebrows. She had her back to the room, shoulders set rigid, hands stuffed in her trouser pockets. Her pixie hairstyle was more of a fade cut, the colour bordering on black. Zello had positioned herself beside a black grand piano, something Tracy assumed was played for entertainment and wasn't just a vast ornament.

Damon closed the door then took out his notepad.

"Shall we sit?" Tracy said, wanting to see Ordsall's face during the interview and not her stiff-as-a-board back.

Rude cow.

Zello sat on one of the sofas, and Ordsall begrudgingly joined her, slumping down and folding her arms over her flat stomach. Tracy and Damon sat on the sofa catty-corner to theirs.

"If you could start from the beginning?" Tracy gave one of her tight smiles.

"This is better coming from you, Chrissy," Zello said. "After all, it *was* your error, wasn't it."

Sting much?

Ordsall blanched, blinked a few times, then stared at a point above Tracy's head. "I got all the patients into bed before eight. They usually go at nine, but I wanted the staff to have an easy night as Mrs Roberts had been playing up the past couple of days."

"Mrs Roberts is . . . ?" Tracy asked, making out she didn't know. She cocked her head.

"The missing resident." Ordsall sniffed.

"Define 'playing up' for me."

"Refusing to obey the rules — you know, not coming to the dining room for dinner, going off on walkabouts in the grounds without telling anyone . . . The list is endless."

"Go on."

"I then made all the nurses a cup of tea. Mrs Roberts wouldn't get into bed, so I left her room to make us the drinks. Nurse Matthews nipped along to check all the residents were truly asleep — they were. Mrs Roberts must have got into bed by herself."

"So Nurse Matthews was the last to see all the residents, was she?"

"He. Nurse Matthews is a he. Yes."

"What happened next?"

"We started watching the film, ate doughnuts — someone had gone out and bought them, no idea who — and by halfway through the movie we . . . uh . . . we'd all fallen asleep." Ordsall's cheeks reddened further. "As I say, that was halfway through, so about tennish."

Zello huffed out a long breath. "This is what happens when you don't get enough sleep during the day before a night shift, Chrissy. I've told all of you this so many times."

Ordsall ignored her. "We woke about one, long after the film had ended. Nurse Matthews went to check the rooms again and found Mrs Roberts gone."

"What did you all do then?"

"We searched the premises first, then the grounds. Nurse Matthews opted to stay inside with the residents." Ordsall slid Zello a sly look. "We're not allowed to leave them alone in the house."

"You're not allowed to nod off either," Zello muttered.

"What time did you call the police?" Tracy asked.

"Around two thirty, after our search." Ordsall shrugged. "We made a terrible mistake by falling asleep . . ."

"You did, but we all trip up every now and then." Tracy directed her attention to Zello. "Does Mrs Roberts have any reason to have left?"

"No." Zello rubbed her forehead. "She's usually a quiet kind of woman, nervy, so I can't for the life of me think why she's gone off like this."

I don't think she went off . . .

"Do you have a photo of her I can look at?" Tracy asked.

"There's one in her room." Zello jumped up, seemingly relieved at having an excuse to leave.

They sat in silence while she was gone, Ordsall staring out at the lawn again, her eyes glassy. Tracy opted not to speak to her — the woman must be beside herself.

She will be if Mrs Roberts turns out to be the dead body.

Zello returned and handed Tracy a photograph.

Shit.

"Is her son still here?" Tracy asked.

Zello nodded. "The chap out in the foyer in the suit."

"I'll be needing to speak to him next."

CHAPTER FOUR

Zello ushered Mrs Roberts' son in and hovered by the door.

"Thank you," Tracy said to her. "I'd rather speak to Mr Roberts alone."

Zello appeared affronted but left with Ordsall, closing the door with a sharp click.

Tracy smiled at Mr Roberts. "Please, take a seat." She waited until he'd sat in the place Ordsall had vacated. "Mr Roberts, I'm DI Tracy Collier, and this is my partner, DS Damon Hanks. We're terribly sorry to meet you under such circumstances." She was getting better at this compassion lark. Pleased with herself, she went on. "When was the last time you saw your mother?"

"Yesterday. About four thirty. I popped in before a work do." He rubbed his hands down his face again like he had in the foyer. His stubble rasped.

"How did she seem to you?"

"Oh, she had a lot to say about the staff. She was unhappy with the way they were treating her."

"How so?"

"She said they wouldn't let her do what she wanted, that she had to follow rules. I said the rules were there for a reason, and she said she didn't like them. Last time she went like this, it was her meds. The dose wasn't high enough."

"What are the meds for?"

"Well, these ones are for her anxiety, but she also has to have insulin."

Tracy made a mental note to ask Gilbert about that after he'd done the post-mortem. "And why was she anxious?"

"She always has been." Mr Roberts sighed. "As far back as I can remember anyway. Always fretting about one thing or another. The circle of worry, that's what she suffers with. Everything goes round and round in her head until she convinces herself bad things will happen. Always has a negative outlook. Even something as small as going to the shop would give her the idea she'd get run over on the way."

"That's terribly sad — and debilitating, I would imagine."

"Most definitely. She ended up a recluse before she came here, and even now she's not much better, preferring to stay in her room instead of mixing with the others." He closed his eyes for a brief moment. "I have no idea where she would have gone. I'd like to think she'd have come to me, but even the idea of her leaving this place has alarm bells ringing. She wouldn't step outside unless she absolutely had to, no matter how much she says she doesn't enjoy it here."

"Hmm. Nurse Ordsall mentioned your mother going out into the grounds recently without asking for permission."

"That doesn't ring true, sorry to say. Mum simply wouldn't do that. She said the woods out the back had wolves in it." He flushed at that. "She might have been losing her mind a bit the last few months."

"That must be very difficult for you to witness."

He nodded. "It is."

"So, do you think someone came in here and took her?" Tracy studied his face for signs of guilt.

She didn't find any.

"What?" he said. "Why would anyone want to come in and take an old lady?" He frowned, eyes glistening. "I can't fathom it. Surely that isn't what happened, is it?"

"Well, if she wouldn't go outside . . ." Tracy let that hang for a heartbeat or two. "I'm not sure what else to think."

He blew out a breath. "I can't imagine . . . I mean, who *does* that to the elderly — or anyone, come to that?"

You'd be surprised . . .

"You've already established your alibi, which we'll obviously be checking, but given the time it was discovered your mother was gone — what time did you leave the party?"

"Three in the morning, and I remember it exactly because I thought how the night had flown and that the last time I'd checked my watch it had been a quarter past midnight."

"So what did you do when you left?"

"Look, I realise why you're asking me these questions, but I assure you, it wasn't me who took my mother out of here. We can't cope with her at our place, what with us working and having kids, so deliberately coming here to get her isn't anything we'd do."

Tracy nodded. "Answer the question, please."

He sighed, and a lock of his hair flew upwards. "I went to an all-night garage to pick up some paracetamol — knew I'd have a bloody great headache come the morning. Too many glasses of wine. I then went home, arriving at approximately three thirty. My answerphone light was flashing, so I listened to the messages, heard the one about Mum, and came straight here."

"Easily verified." Tracy had a thought. "Did you drive home from the party yourself?"

"No, I took a taxi, which picked me up outside about five past three. Tina's Cabs. You can check. A driver called Bob. He told me all about his daughter making it into uni. Her name is Xanthia, and I remember it because it's unusual. Once I heard the voice message, I rang Tina's. Bob turned up again and left me here about three fifty, which can be backed up by staff."

"We'll be looking into it, yes." Tracy didn't believe for one minute Mr Roberts was responsible. His answers had flowed, and he'd shown no signs of distress at being questioned, just about the fact his mother had gone missing.

His mother is dead.

"Mr Roberts, I have some upsetting news. We were called out this morning to view a body a few miles along the road there." She held up her hand to stop him talking. "Going by the picture Mrs Zello showed me of your mother, I have reason to believe the body may be hers."

He stared, mouth opening and closing.

"Would you mind looking at an image I have to confirm whether it is your mother?" she asked softly.

"Oh God . . . A *dead* woman's picture?" He swallowed then stood to pace in front of the sofa. "I'm . . . I'm not sure I can stand to look at something like that."

"I'm afraid you'll have to — unless you have a sibling or a father who can do it?"

"No," he said, shaking his head. "Only child, and Dad died a few years back. Oh, bloody hell . . ." He pinched his bottom lip.

"The sooner we know if it *is* your mother, the sooner we can crack on with our investigation and find out who did it. Isn't that what you want, Mr Roberts?" She slid her phone out of her pocket and accessed her images folder. The woman looked extremely dead, and Tracy shuddered. "This may be a shock for you, so please brace yourself, sir."

She walked to him, wine fumes coming off him, that scent all people had when they'd sunk a few too many. She held out the phone so the screen faced him.

His wail of anguish hurt Tracy's heart, and she wondered when she'd even *got* that heart. Was he crying out because it was his mother or because he stared at the image of a deceased woman and couldn't seem to tear his gaze away?

"Jesus Christ." He flopped onto the sofa, propped his elbows on his knees, and covered his face. Then the sobs came, and his shoulders shook.

Uncomfortable in the face of such grief, Tracy walked backwards until she reached the other sofa. She sat beside

Damon, who held her hand for a second or two then got up to park himself beside Mr Roberts.

"Is it your mother?" Damon asked, placing a hand on Mr Roberts' shoulder.

Tracy knew it was, but confirmation was needed.

"Yes." The word was broken into two parts, raspy and filled with the echo of loss.

"I'm so sorry," Tracy said. "Is there anyone who can come to collect you?" She was mindful he probably still had a couple of bottles of wine surging through his system and shouldn't be driving yet.

"My wife . . ."

"Was she at home while you were at the work party?" Tracy asked.

"Yes, with the children, and her friend came round for the evening." He lowered his hands. "She's going to be devastated. My mother was a mum to her, too."

Shit.

"I'll ask someone to give her a call, shall I?" Tracy offered.

"No. No, it's fine. I'll do it now." He rose and walked over to the window, wiping his face with his fingertips.

Tracy jerked her head at Damon, indicating they should leave to give Mr Roberts some privacy. Outside in the hallway, Mr Roberts' choked-out words filtered through the door, and Tracy scrunched her eyes shut, wishing she was anywhere but here.

"This is bloody awful," Damon said quietly, rubbing his forehead.

"It always is." She opened her eyes and stared at the wall opposite. "Now we just have to find out how the hell she got herself killed and why anyone would want to do that to her."

"Lots of staff to interview." He let out a long sigh.

"Yes. No time like the present, I suppose. I just need to check Mr Roberts is all right first." She dipped her head inside the room. He wasn't on the phone but studied the ceiling while sitting on the sofa he'd used before. "Is your wife on her way?"

He glanced over, eyes red, the same as his nose. "Yes. The kids are at school, so she's coming right over."

"Will you be okay on your own until she gets here?"

He stood and walked towards her. "Yes. I'm going to wait at reception so I can see her as soon as she gets here."

"Okay. We'll go with you, but please don't mention your mother's death to anyone here." She led the way to the foyer and left him staring through the window that overlooked the driveway. Then she strode to the desk. "Hi." She smiled. "Sorry to trouble you again." She wasn't sorry at all, but it was the sort of thing you said, wasn't it. "Do you also have someone manning this desk at night?"

"No, just daytimes."

"Okay. Is Nurse Matthews still here?"

The receptionist grimaced. "Over there in the corner. Harry, his name is. He's blaming himself as he's the one who went in and found Mrs Roberts gone."

"Thanks."

Tracy observed Matthews for a moment, trying to get his measure. He didn't seem anything but distraught, knuckling his eyes then staring out of the window, bottom lip wobbling. He appeared genuine enough, but looks could be deceiving, and many a killer was a good actor.

So she didn't seem weird just gawping, Tracy joined the upset nurse. "Harry Matthews?"

The man nodded.

Tracy showed her ID. "We need to question you, I'm afraid."

Matthews swallowed hard.

"The receiving room, please." Tracy followed him there, Damon beside her.

"This has got to be awful for him," he whispered, nodding at Matthews' back.

"Not if he did it," Tracy said under her breath. "Then again, it could be awful. He might be thinking he'll get caught."

Damon pursed his lips. "Fucking hell."

"Exactly. I'm leaning more towards innocent at the moment."

"Okay. I'll see if I can pick up any tells while you talk to him."

"You and me both."

Once they were all inside the room, Tracy closed the door and told Matthews to sit where Mr Roberts had. The position was ideal — she could watch him closely for signs of guilt. The only guilt on display was that of a man who was chastising himself for falling asleep and allowing himself to let a patient go missing, even though it wasn't necessarily his responsibility but Ordsall's.

Matthews corroborated Ordsall's version of events, and once Tracy had finished interviewing him, they moved on to all the other nurses who had been around last night. Everyone said exactly the same thing.

Either they were telling the truth or they'd concocted a story that each nurse spilled out as though from a script.

Tracy was no closer to finding the truth, and she seethed, leaving the care home with a bee in her bonnet and a worm of unease wiggling in her belly. Something was off, and she was determined to discover what it was.

CHAPTER FIVE

Last Night

He found her in a bit of a state. He'd forgotten to leave her a bucket, but considering she has her wrists and ankles tied, she wouldn't have been able to use it anyway.

She's got shit seeping through her skinny jeans. A dirty girl, that's what she is, and he's not just talking about the mess she's made. Girls like her boil his piss, asking for sex and expecting something in return for it. They should be thrown inside a small room and locked up until they learn their lesson.

Ironic.

She stares up at him, and he stares back, pleased by her frown. She hasn't recognised him from when he'd brought her here, and that's exactly what he wants.

"What . . . who are you?" she asks, eyes wide.

"What on earth are you doing down here?" He looks at her as though he's never seen her before in his life.

"Someone . . . another man . . . he brought me here and left me."

"Goodness, that's just terrible. And you're all tied up, too. Have you had an accident?" He waves at her jeans.

"I . . . I couldn't hold it."

"Deary me. Wait there while I get you something to wear." He leaves the room, laughing because she can't exactly go anywhere, can she. He hangs around in the corridor for a bit, having already brought the clean clothes here earlier. He scoops them up then goes back to her, helping her to stand. "Let's get you washed."

He leads her out then down the corridor to a long-abandoned shower room that thankfully still has hot running water. "Now, don't go galloping off when I untie you, all right? I'm just here to help, I promise."

She nods, and he sets her free. While she undresses, seemingly unperturbed by him being there, he turns the shower on, and once she's under the spray, she uses the liquid soap hanging from the curtain rail. He gathers her soiled clothing and pops it into a carrier bag for dealing with later.

Clean now, she dries using a white towel then slips on the grey tracksuit he gave her. All the while, they don't speak. Her teeth chatter from the cold — no heating on here — and he wonders whether they'll clack together from fear later.

She stands there, waiting for instructions, and he smiles.

"Now, I'm going to tie you up again while I leave for a moment because I really have no idea who you are, all right? You really shouldn't be here. It's private property."

Her mouth opens in a large O. She nods, and her eyes have a glint of terror in them, as though what's going on is something that's happened to her before.

Is she frightened of what might occur next?

He binds her wrists and ankles, then leaves.

* * *

Back in the shower room, looking different yet again — lighter hair, a beard, and a change of clothes — he advances towards her, swaggering to appear menacing. She retreats, stepping back so quickly she meets with the wall. Gripping her arm, he yanks her towards the door.

She opens her mouth to speak, but he can't be having that.

"Shh. Not a sound, right?" It comes out as a snarl, and he loves it.

She nods frantically.

"You do everything I say, and I'll let you go." He squeezes her elbow to see if she'll squeal.

She doesn't.

Good.

He unties her, stuffs the rope in his pocket, then leads the way to the main building. None of the others will hear him — their doughnuts were laced with the powder from inside sleeping capsules, just enough of a dusting to give him the window of time he needs. Down the hallway they go to Mrs Roberts' room. He needs to get this done fast before the old dear goes stiff.

"Run your fingers through your hair," he says.

Dirty Girl frowns but does it. A few strands and a knotted tangle break free, draping over her knuckle.

"Put them on the pillow." He holds his breath in case she freaks, and his heartbeat speeds — he feels sick with the pressure of it all.

She stares at him, as though she'd like to kill him, but places her hair beside Mrs Roberts' head. It looks like a giant spider with only one long leg. He nods, pleased with her compliance.

"Now press your fingertips on the bedside cabinet," he orders.

She does.

"Good."

Sweeping the dead weight of the insufferable Mrs Roberts into his arms, he jerks his head for his captive to follow, and she does, walking at a swift pace until she's by his side.

Why didn't she run in the other direction? At least try to get away?

Out in the rear staff car park, he dumps Mrs Roberts in the back of his vehicle then ushers Dirty Girl into the passenger seat, cuffing her wrist to the inside handle. Then he gets in and leans towards her.

"Now, as you know, your hair and fingerprints are at a crime scene, so if you don't listen to me and don't do what I want, you'll be framed for that old biddy's murder, meaning, I won't remove the hair and prints when I get back, got it?"

She nods again, inhaling air through her nose, nostrils flaring.

He sets off, happy Blooming Age is in the middle of nowhere and no one is likely to be about. A few miles down the road, he turns off onto an access track that leads to a farm. Engine and lights off, he leaves the car, collects Mrs Roberts, engages the locks, then takes her across a field, over the width of a path, and dumps her on the other side next to a hedge.

Back at the car, he unlocks Dirty Girl's cuff and hauls her out, dragging her with him to Mrs Roberts. "Right then. Watch this. It's what'll happen to you if you disobey me."

He has to do something to ensure she doesn't leg it — there's something he needs her to do in a minute.

Lifting Mrs Roberts and leaning her back against his front, he whips out his hunting knife then slits the bitch's throat. He wishes she wasn't already dead and he could have watched her blood spurting everywhere, but you can't have everything, and he ought to be grateful he has something.

Beggars can't be choosers. Mum used to say that.

Dirty Girl makes a strange sound, a cross between a whimper and laughter, and he imagines she's nervous and scared and doesn't know her arse from her elbow.

"You . . ." she manages then clamps her lips tight, as if remembering he'd told her not to make a sound.

He places Mrs Roberts back on the ground, curling her into the foetal position, and it looks like she's just fallen asleep — if it wasn't for the gaping slit in her neck.

"Spit on her," he says.

Dirty Girl backs away, turning to run, but he's quick enough and catches hold of her arm before she has a chance to scarper.

"That wasn't . . . sensible," he whispers, yanking her along with him, back to Mrs Roberts. "I said, spit on her."

Instead, she spits on his forehead, and it takes all his strength to hold back from smacking her cheek. She stares at him, her face showcased by the moonlight, and it seems to him she has hate brewing inside her and wants to grab his knife and gut him.

That won't be happening.

He scoops the spit off with a fingertip then lets it drip onto Mrs Roberts' chin. "There. All done anyway, despite you defying me."

He brings his knife up, ready to stab at her, and she catches sight of it, her eyes widening — not with fear now but something he'd swear was jealousy that he's holding it and not her. He jabs it forward, but she grips his wrist, surprisingly strong for her size, and the blade edges its way towards his neck.

They struggle, him fighting to push her backwards, the pair of them moving more than a few paces, and even though he's bigger and taller, it feels as though she has the upper hand.

White noise enters his head, and he shoves her. She loses her balance, and he wrestles his arm out of her grip and slashes out at her, slicing the pad of her thumb. She staggers past him, one step, two steps, three, four, five, until she runs towards the dead old bitch. He chases after her, adrenaline spiking, needing to get hold of her so she doesn't make it out onto the road. She disappears through the hedge, creating a wide gap, and he pulls her backwards. They almost topple over the body, and she manages to get away from him again and runs towards the path. Then she's on it, heading for the road, and he scarpers after her, lunging out onto the verge, but she's gone, she's fucking gone.

He searches for ten minutes in the hedges but can't spare any more time. If the others wake up and he's not there . . .

He heads for the access road and jumps in his car, gets back to the room he'd kept Dirty Girl in, removing his clothing and stashing it away in an old cupboard along with the outfit he'd used when he'd brought her here, among others. He redresses then takes the bag of her filthy, shit-stained clothes and rushes out into the back garden, scattering her things over the grass. The carrier bag he takes back inside and shoves it into the recently purchased incinerator. With a quick check to make sure Dirty Girl's spider hair is still on the pillow — it is — he goes and join the others, who are still snoring in front of the TV.

Settling into a chair, he closes his eyes, thinking it would be as well that he also has a nap. It'll make it more authentic when someone else wakes and finds him sleeping.

As he drifts off, he thinks about how he's going to have to find Dirty Girl all over again and shut her the fuck up for good.

CHAPTER SIX

Tracy sat on the edge of Nada's desk after contacting SOCO to go out to Blooming Age and do a sweep for any evidence that may have been left behind. "So, nothing on Mrs Roberts except what we already know — elderly lady, lived in a care home, had diabetes and severe anxiety. No priors, not a bad word to be said about her from the people you contacted. That right, Nada?"

"Yes, boss. But Mr Roberts, her son — Frankie — was arrested for disorderly conduct in eighty-nine. Just a kid at the time, and he hasn't done anything wrong since, not even so much as a parking ticket. The arrest was for a bit of a scuffle in a youth centre, that was all. Two lads started on him, he fought back."

"Okay. I didn't have a feeling it was anything to do with him when we spoke," Tracy said, "but that doesn't mean anything. My gut instinct could be broken today."

"My head's broken," Alastair said.

"Too many bevvies last night, was it?" Tracy asked.

Everyone laughed, and it was nice to hear. The team worked hard and deserved a bit of light-heartedness every now and then. Not too much, though, or they'd get jack shit done.

"No, I banged my head on the top of the doorframe," Alastair said, rubbing it for effect.

"But you're a short-arse. How the hell did you do that?" Tracy asked.

Alastair blushed. "I'd rather not say."

"Something kinky going on, was there?" Tim raised his eyebrows.

"Not bloody likely," Alastair said.

Much as the teasing was enjoyable, Tracy needed them to get on with the job. "Sorry to break this up, guys, but we have a dead woman to get some justice for, so we need to move on." She paused. "Anything else, Nada?"

"Mrs Roberts, Frankie's wife — Polly — is clean. We've been digging about on their social media, and Frankie and Polly present themselves as your usual married couple with kids. All posts are positive and happy, but not the kind of happy where you can tell people are making out life is great when really it's crap."

"I was just going to ask that," Tracy said. "So much of social media is lies." *A bit like my life.* "So, we're not really any further forward, are we. Shit." She rammed a hand through her hair. "Right, I'm going to get in contact with the officers who turned up at Blooming Age first, see if they have any information we haven't. I'll be back in a sec."

Tracy left the incident room and took the stairs to the front desk. If she didn't lose weight with all that climbing up and going down, she'd blow a gasket.

The waiting area was surprisingly empty, so she leant on the desk and jerked her head at Vic. He strolled over, cup in hand, grin in place. She liked him.

"What can I do you for, boss?"

"You're not doing me for anything, mate." She grinned. "On a serious note, I want to know who went out to the Blooming Age care home in the early hours. I need to have a word."

"Give us a sec and I'll tell you." He put his cup down and tapped on the keyboard on the desk. "The poor sods are still there."

"What, the PCs I saw there earlier have been there since they were called out? That doesn't sound right. No shift change?"

Vic shrugged. "Got a note on here that they requested to stay."

"Hmm. Get one on the phone for me, will you?"

While she waited for Vic to make contact, Tracy walked around the waiting area and stopped short. She hadn't had time to take note before, but Lisa's EFIT was tacked at the top of an information board with the caption: HAVE YOU SEEN THIS WOMAN? Tracy's stomach churned. Of *course* the image would be there and in any police station close to the one in the city. Especially as Lisa was believed to have slit the throat of a police chief. Tracy shuddered and turned her back on her sister's likeness, unable to stand looking at it anymore.

Unable to stand being reminded of the lies.

"Right, boss. Here you go." Vic handed the phone over. "James Quinn for you."

"Thanks." Tracy put the phone to her ear. "Hi, James, DI Tracy Collier. I just wanted to touch base to see what went on during the night after you arrived. I should have asked you while I was there earlier." *But I forgot, for fuck's sake.* So much for her action sheets. She didn't even follow them herself.

"Hello, ma'am. Everyone on scene was interviewed, and while that was going on, I had a look around. I found some dirty clothing on the back lawn so got that photographed then packed up as possible evidence. No one there had seen it before; it didn't belong to any nurses or residents."

Tracy frowned. "Hmm. Wonder what it was doing there then?"

"No idea. It belongs to a woman — or I assume it does anyway, going by the sizing."

"Why did you choose to stick around? You know, pull a double shift?"

"Could have been my nan, ma'am. I just felt the need to see it through instead of leaving it to the next lot."

"That's nice of you. I take it the evidence — the clothing — has been sent in already?"

"Um, no."

She imagined him wincing.

"Where is it?" she asked, her stomach rolling.

"I've locked it in a safe in the manager's office."

"Christ. That's a bit of a mistake, isn't it, but I'll pretend I know nothing about it and come and pick it up myself, okay?"

"Thanks, ma'am. What with everything going on . . . it was so busy with all the nurses, and some residents woke up because of the noise. Bloody chaos for a while, it was."

"Next time, call for someone to collect it if you can't leave the scene."

"Will do. Thanks, ma'am."

"For what?"

"You know . . ."

"I have no idea what you're talking about." She smiled, feeling stupid for it, because he couldn't even sodding see her.

"Err, yes, ma'am."

"SOCO might get to you before me. I've not long asked them to go down there."

"What are they needed for, ma'am, if you don't mind me asking?"

"Mrs Roberts was found dead this morning. Please keep that to yourself. I don't want anyone who was there at the time to be aware we know."

"D'you think it was someone *here*?" He sounded gobsmacked.

"It's possible. We can't discount any theory at the moment."

"Blimey."

"Okay, let's get off the phone now. I'll be there in a bit. This is as much my fault as it is yours, by the way, that thing I'm not telling anyone about. I should have spoken to you while I was there, but I got caught up myself, so I know how it goes."

"You're very kind, ma'am."

Don't you believe it. I'm covering my own arse as well as yours. I'm a selfish bitch, no point pretending I'm not.

"No problem. Catch you soon."

She called Damon to ask him to tell the team they were going back to the care home and for him to join her downstairs. She gave Vic the phone, thanked him, then headed for her car, thinking Damon would gather where she'd gone. Inside, she had a look at herself in the rearview mirror. Someone stood there behind her car, a woman with purple hair and thick-lens specs. Tracy's stomach muscles contracted, and her heartrate kicked into overdrive.

What the fuck?

She jumped out, dashing towards the back of the car, but the woman had gone.

Not just a woman. Lisa. With purple hair this time?

Tracy frantically walked around the parking area, peering inside each vehicle in case Lisa was in one of them. She wasn't, so Tracy ran to the entrance and glanced up and down the road. No one, not even a cyclist.

Christ . . .

Adrenaline rush fading, she semi-staggered towards the station door, needing a drink to soothe her suddenly parched throat. She pushed inside, intent on getting to the toilet, but Damon came flying around the corner from the stairwell.

"Hi," Tracy managed, the word breathy. "Ready?"

"Yep. Sorry I took so long. The farmer called. Wanted to know when he could use his field again."

"Hmm, that's one for SOCO to answer." She moved to the desk.

"On it, boss," Vic said.

"Earwigging, were you?" She smiled.

"Bit hard not to when you're both talking loudly."

"Get you." She laughed and nipped to the loo to wet her throat. Back in reception, she clicked her thumb and finger at Damon and left the station, amazed at how chameleon-like she was, changing moods so quickly. Covering up. Lying.

Damon strode beside her. "Any reason for going back, or did your gut start talking to you and you've got one of those hunches we're meant to always have?"

"All my gut's saying is that I forgot to eat breakfast. We need to collect something at the care home." She got into the car.

"Oh yeah?" Damon said, sitting beside her and securing his safety belt.

"Yes." She started the engine then set off. "Keep this between us, obviously . . . I don't want to get the officer in the shit because it means plunging myself in it, too, but—"

"Bugger. Did you drop the ball?"

"I did. From a great height. Not only did I forget to speak to the uniforms at the home earlier, but James Quinn, one of the PCs, found evidence, and since he was so busy, he bagged it and put it in the manager's safe."

"Shit."

"Exactly that. I told him we'll pick it up and say no more about it. I should have been more diligent." She sighed. "More and more lately, I'm fucking up."

"Let it go," he said. "It's tough being in your position. Have you got anything on your mind? You haven't been quite the same since—"

"I'm fine." *Don't go there, Damon.* "I'm just a tetchy cow, you know that. Sometimes I'm up, sometimes I'm down, and if you're *really* lucky, most times I'm in between." She glanced over and smiled, hoping he'd forget what he'd been about to say. "I'm just glad, once again, that I twigged what I hadn't done so I can fix it. I'm getting on my own nerves with this bad memory business."

"Well, you're not getting on mine, so that's a bonus."

She laughed. "One day I will."

"Maybe."

They continued without speaking. That was the best thing about being with Damon. He didn't expect her to talk all the time, to fill what some might say were awkward silences. She mulled over why her brain tended to skip over some things, why there seemed to be a black hole in her head where important information disappeared, only to come out again when she was either occupied with something else or it woke her from sleep.

Maybe my head's too full all the time. Maybe that mind box of mine needs emptying.

To be free, she'd need a therapist, and she didn't fancy doing that again. Did she? Dr F had led her down a path that had revealed far more than she'd bargained for in the Past. She couldn't imagine what another stint of sessions would produce. Things she'd forgotten about because they were too traumatic to remember? What if there were far more things that had happened to her, and she had no idea because her mind had confiscated them to save her sanity? She had to admit, she'd felt better somehow after telling Dr F about the rainbow scarf day and how she'd burnt her leg on the three-bar fire as a kid. Would talking about *everything* cure her? Make her a nicer person?

"I might see someone," she blurted.

"Pardon?" Damon scratched his temple. "Did I miss something before you said that?"

"No. I might go and see someone. You know . . ."

"Oh. So you're ready for that?"

"Might be."

"I'll leave you to find the right person and make an appointment this time."

"That would be best, yes."

CHAPTER SEVEN

Tracy turned into the Blooming Age driveway and parked near the front doors, glad that conversation couldn't carry on. The PC who had been outside before had gone, and Simone York had taken his place. They must have wrapped things up at the field, then, for her to be here.

"Hi," Tracy said. "Information blackout regarding Mrs Roberts' body being found this morning, please. No talking to nurses or other staff about it."

"Yes, boss."

Tracy swept inside. "Over here," she told Damon, walking towards the other PC she recognised as being the one who'd stood with Mr Roberts earlier.

He turned and smiled, flushing a little, and ended his conversation with the receptionist to join Tracy in the centre of the foyer. "James Quinn, ma'am."

"Hello, you." She held out a hand, and they shook, more to seal their deal than to make nice. "I'll collect the bags in a bit. Better to keep them locked up for now."

"Okay. I need to chat to that lady there," he said. "She's one of the daytime staff. I'm talking to everyone who came on shift this morning."

"Report anything suspicious to me, all right? I'm going to call a couple of people from my team and ask them to come down and help you out. You must be exhausted."

"Thank you." He walked off and sat beside a woman who had clearly been crying.

Tracy called Nada and requested that she ask Tim and Erica to come and do some questioning. "But I want you to go down and see Gilbert if he's back from the scene."

"Me?" Nada said, a bit on the high-pitched side.

"Yes, you. Aren't you up for that or what?"

"Well, yes, but . . . I just wasn't expecting something so . . ."

"Important?"

"Yes."

"And why's that? You're my right-hand woman. This will give you more experience for when you go for an inspector's exam in the future."

"Oh, I really don't think—"

"I do. You're a brilliant copper." She'd better lower her voice. "I want you to view Mrs Roberts and see if anything springs out at you. It's all a bit off to me, the way she left and ended up in a field. I've got things to do here at the home, otherwise I'd go with you. Take Alastair. He can rub your back if you puke."

"Oh, don't . . ."

"I have to go. I'll be back as soon as I can." She shoved the phone in her pocket.

Catching Zello's attention, Tracy waved, and the woman came stalking over.

"There are people in white jumpsuits walking around," Zello whispered, her eyes darting here and there, as if she was on some kind of covert mission. All she'd need was a magnifying glass and she'd be well away. "It's terribly upsetting for the residents."

"Better that they're here to find evidence so we can collar who . . ." Tracy stopped herself. Then again, wasn't it better to inform the manager about what had happened? "Give me a second."

She turned to find Quinn coming towards her. Tilting her head to one side, she waited for him to follow her to a corner.

"What's up, ma'am?"

"Mrs Zello. Did her alibi check out?"

"Yes. She was at home, family dinner — extended family, too, plus the owner of this place. They stayed up chatting until two, then everyone left. Mrs Zello went to bed, her husband verified it. I know a spouse can cover up for their other half, but we can't prove she wasn't in bed, so . . ."

"Okay. Fine. I'm going to let her know what happened to Mrs Roberts. She might even know if Mr Roberts said something after I left." *What a shit-show. I should have stayed here for a while longer.* "I've got Tim and Erica coming down to lend a hand with the questioning. Together you should get through it quickly. I've got to get on. I'll say goodbye before I go."

She made yet another call to Nada to get her to ask Julia, the family liaison officer, to pay a visit to Mr and Mrs Roberts before their children came home from school. The poor couple probably needed some support.

She returned to the manager and asked if they could talk privately, then crooked her finger at Damon for him to join them.

In her office, Zello wrung her hands while standing beside a large window. Trees swayed at the bottom of the lawn, and SOCOs knelt on the grass, sifting through it. They concentrated beside a pruned bush.

That must be where the clothes were. And shit, there are groundskeepers who could have been involved in this. They'll need to be spoken to.

Damon stood beside Zello and peered out.

"What on *earth* is going on?" Zello jabbed her thumb towards the glass. "This is most unsettling."

Tracy delivered the news in her usual manner. "Mrs Roberts was found dead in a field this morning."

Damon coughed.

Sorry . . .

"Oh . . . dear God . . ." Zello deflated, sinking into her desk chair. "What . . . How . . . ?"

"She died before getting to the field. So she either left here of her own accord, died, and someone slit her throat then took her there or—"

"What?" It came out as a squeak, and Zello's face paled, then the whiteness bloomed with spots of red on her cheeks. She ran a shaking hand through her hair. "Who would want to kill Mrs Roberts? I thought . . . I thought she'd just run off."

"Perhaps she did. Someone may have intercepted her." Tracy approached the desk and remained standing, pressing her fingertips on the surface. "Is there anyone working here who might be a little . . . unpleasant to the residents?"

"What? No!" Zello slapped a palm to her chest. "Do you think I would keep any staff in employment if I thought for one *second* they'd be unpleasant?"

"Of course not. I worded that badly." *I'm so good at that.* "Let me rephrase. Is there anyone you know who may have wanted to harm Mrs Roberts — nurse, cleaner, gardener, her family? Anyone at all who would have come into contact with her."

"No. Absolutely no. That reword was just as bad as the original statement, by the way. Good grief, it's a good job you're not a doctor."

"No bedside manner. I know." Tracy didn't bother smiling. She didn't have the inclination to even fake being pleasant. Zello was winding her up.

Funny how I can dish it out but don't like getting it back.

"Let's talk about Mrs Roberts' behaviour prior to her . . . unfortunate end."

"Yes, she'd been a little unlike her usual self the past couple of days, but nothing that would make someone do *that* to her." She fanned her face with her hand. "I feel quite sick . . ."

"I'd appreciate it if you didn't puke right now. I'd also appreciate it if you could keep what happened to Mrs Roberts to yourself. Even from the nurses. We're not ready yet to give everyone full disclosure. I'm only telling you because of the police presence, which is disruptive to the running of the home. Did you know some clothes were found?"

"Yes, that *nice* policeman asked us if we recognised it. Far too modern for the residents, if a bit grubby and terribly smelly, and I can't imagine any of the nurses slinging their things out on the grass. That in itself is strange, don't you think?"

"Yes. Very. Especially as all the nurses were supposedly asleep, so it begs the question as to who put the clothing there. What disturbs me is how Mrs Roberts got out."

"We lock up at six once I leave, but we don't set the alarm until after the residents are in bed at nine — we do a final check to make sure everyone is present and accounted for first. Unfortunately, that task seems to have been ignored because everyone fell asleep. I'm so angry about that."

"Will they get written warnings?" *Because they bloody should.*

"Definitely."

Tracy nodded. "Good. I'm a bit miffed at the fact that people pay hard-earned money to ensure their family members are safe here and, well, they're not, are they."

Zello's head moved back sharply, reminding Tracy of an emu. "There are rules in place. They weren't followed. That will be dealt with swiftly, I assure you."

"I hope so. It wouldn't surprise me if some people moved their mothers and fathers elsewhere once this gets out."

Zello's eyes widened. "Oh. I hadn't thought of that."

Tracy sighed. "Well, I'll be sending some of my team round to the nurses' houses later to be questioned again. Best to be extra thorough. I take it you can give me their addresses — all the staff actually. Cleaners, the people who cut the grass. Everyone."

"I can do that for you now."

While Zello busied herself gathering the information, Tracy left the room, Damon behind her. She had SOCO to talk to.

Out on the patio that ran the length of the building in front of the back lawn, Tracy took in the scene as if she were the killer — *if* the killer had abducted Mrs Roberts first and had exited this way.

"What do you reckon, Damon? Would he have come through the door we just used or one of the others along the way there?"

An officer in whites dusted one of the handles for prints, while another knelt on the patio, digging out something from the moss between two.

"God knows. Coming out this way seems sensible. Less chance of being seen carrying a dead body."

"So you think she was killed here, do you?" She cocked her head.

"Just a figure of speech. Whether she was dead or not, it'd be best not to draw attention to yourself by going out the front, wouldn't it?"

"Let's face it, there isn't much traffic out there in the day, so nighttime would be even less. It was dark. All they'd have done was wait for any cars to go past then get on with it. Yes?" She looked at him.

"We'll find out soon enough once forensics have worked it out."

"Hmm." She called an officer over — one by the bush — so she didn't step on the grass. "Hi, Ben, how's it going?"

"Not too bad. Should be here for about another three or four hours." He lowered a mask from his mouth.

"Anything I can use here? Any information?"

"We've found a few of those sticky balls from undergrowth. Do you know the kind I mean? I can't think of the plant's bloody name."

Tracy nodded.

"They're not consistent with this garden," Ben said. "As you can see, this is well cared for. Those types of weeds aren't here."

Might have been on the clothes?

Ben's eyebrows shot up. "Oh, and we also found some hair on the deceased's pillow — black. Long."

"Right. Bit weird considering the victim's is short and grey-white." Tracy frowned.

"It is. That's been sent off already — thought it best we get the guys going on it sooner rather than later."

"Yes, thanks."

"There was also a clump of mud beside the bush. Different colour to what's in the flowerbeds, so I'm assuming it also didn't come from this garden. Testing will prove that one way or the other."

"Okay, thanks, Ben. I need to be getting back to the station. See you soon."

Ben replaced the mask and got on with his work. Tracy walked inside with Damon, heading for Zello's office. The door was open, so they stepped in.

"Here you go," Zello said, holding out a piece of paper with names, addresses, and phone numbers printed on it.

Tracy folded it and slid it in her pocket. "Thanks. I'll need the bags from out of the safe."

"Oh. Yes. Right. Such a strange thing to do, leaving clothes out there." Zello walked over to a waist-high safe and twisted the dial on the front — left, left, right.

"Why such a big safe?" Tracy asked.

"We keep the residents' valuables in here. You know, rings, necklaces, their spending money."

"Spending money?"

"Yes, there's a van that comes round once a week, a mobile shop, and everyone buys what they want there. Sweets, snacks, books, things like that."

"What's the name of the company?" Tracy glanced at Damon and gestured for him to get his notebook out.

"Shop on the Go." Zello opened the safe and took the bags out.

Damon tucked them under his arm. "And the person who runs it?"

"Martin," Zello said. "I just know him as Martin."

Tracy resisted rolling her eyes. "So, another security lapse, maybe?"

Zello locked the safe then turned, her cheeks flushed. "It seems so." She appeared crestfallen, genuinely upset. "I didn't think . . ."

"You'd benefit from a security course, something like that," Tracy said. "Anyone could come along with a van, chat to the residents, find out if they're worth a bob or two."

"Christ, do you think . . . ?"

"You can never be too careful in life, Mrs Zello — you can't be too careful with *other people's* lives either." *Says the woman who let her sister go free to kill again.*

"Are you blaming *me*?" Zello's eyes watered.

"I'm not doing anything of the sort." *I tell so many lies.* "Just pointing out where things could be tightened up in the future." Tracy paused. "So this sort of thing doesn't happen again."

She strode out, not in the mood to get into an argument with the woman — and that was where it would go if Tracy remained. Zello would most probably want to defend herself, but the fact was plain that someone had taken Mrs Roberts from here, or the woman had walked away, and no one had known for hours.

Not good enough.

In a private corner, she rang Nada to check out the company Shop on the Go and find out who the hell this Martin bloke was.

As if they needed more suspects than they already had.

CHAPTER EIGHT

He'd sped away from the care home and made straight for the car wash, wanting to get rid of anything that might have got on the vehicle during his little nighttime jaunt.

He's in his garage now, hoovering the car's interior, especially the back seat where the old dear had been. He can't be doing with skin cells or hair being left behind.

Job done, he goes into the house and thinks over the past few hours. Once Mrs Roberts' disappearance had been discovered, all hell had broken loose with nurses muttering about losing their jobs for falling asleep. No mention of an elderly resident being gone, not at first. Then the enormity of it all had kicked in, and he'd watched them, fascinated, as they'd scurried around trying to find her.

He'd offered to check the unused wing. While there, he'd made sure nothing was amiss from storing Dirty Girl there. Luckily, later, when the police had arrived, they'd been more interested in finding Mrs Roberts, not a bag of men's clothes, which he'd put in the incinerator before the authorities had arrived. Many a soiled sheet went in there, the material burning to ash.

The officer who'd spotted Dirty Girl's outfit in the garden had stared at it for a while and had appeared ethereal for a moment, bathed as he was by the outside wall light casting its glow on him. The items had been placed in clear plastic bags then shown to all the nurses.

Things had gone exactly to plan.

Except for Dirty Girl getting away. He'll have to fix that later, no time now. He needs a shower to remove any evidence from his body.

CHAPTER NINE

I wake to the sound of the doorbell twanging on my last nerve. I've barely had five hours of sleep, and my mind takes a moment to catch up. Tendrils of memory float inside my head, something about last night, a terrible thing happening, something to do with me, then it all comes tumbling back. Someone had taken Mrs Roberts, and my main concern is that they'll suspect me. I've been a little short with her lately, what with her antics, and once people really think about it, they'll remember how I've been acting around the old woman and tell someone.

I stumble out of bed, and the door chimes again, seeming louder, more urgent. I grab my peach-coloured dressing gown that smells manky and drag it on, then go to the front door. There's no glass in it, so I can't see the shape of anyone there. I look through the peephole.

Shit. It's those police officers from earlier.

My heart pounds, and a lump sits at the back of my throat.

I open the door and smile, lips twitching with the nerves kicking in. Are they here to accuse me? I haven't done anything wrong except to snap at Mrs Roberts, so surely they're not here to arrest me or anything.

Unless you can be arrested for sleeping at work.

"Ah, Miss Ordsall," the woman says — Tracy something or other. "May we come in? Sorry if we just got you out of bed. I appreciate you can't have had much sleep. Are you back at Blooming Age tonight?"

"No." I blink, for some reason surprised it's getting dark out. Is it even the same day? *Wake the hell up*. "Mrs Zello has let us skip a night to catch up. What do you want?"

"Oh, we're interviewing everyone again — formally this time. Everyone who was there last night when Mrs Roberts went missing. Nothing to worry about."

Right. So it *is* the same day.

I step back and allow them to enter, then lead them into the living room. "Do you want any tea?" *I need one.*

"No, thank you. We'll sit down, though, if you don't mind."

"Oh. Sorry. I'm not used to visitors." *Never was any good at making friends*. "Yes, you have a seat. There." I point to the brown, old-fashioned sofa, then scratch my head, wondering if it would be rude to go and make myself a drink.

The female officer hands over a card, and I stare at it, a bit dumbfounded. Collier, that's her surname.

"That's in case you need to contact me," Collier says, parking her backside. "You know, if you remember anything after we've left. Oftentimes, people get random memories way down the line, so if you recall anything else, you can use those numbers."

"Right. Thank you." I clutch the card, and my hand shakes.

"You okay?" the man asks.

Damon Hanks. I remember that name.

"Um, I haven't had enough sleep." I'd planned to get at least twelve hours in, but these two have fucked that up. "I'll just make myself a cuppa. That'll wake me up."

I go into the kitchen before they have a chance to stop me, popping the card under a magnet on the fridge. I make my tea quickly, using my instant water heater rather than the kettle. While I add sugar and stir in milk, I think about last night.

I was the one who was supposed to have got Mrs Roberts to bed, but she'd messed me about, and someone else had done it — although none of the other nurses are admitting to it.

Why is that? They're going to think I'm lying about not putting her to bed. They'll say it was me and I'm covering up.

But I swear, I haven't done anything wrong.

I take my cup into the living room and sit on the edge of one of the chairs that matches the sofa. The suite is my mother's, and it reminds me of my childhood, something I don't want to remember all that often.

"Okay," Collier says. "Go through what happened again."

While Mr Hanks writes what I'm saying on an official-looking form, I repeat what I told her last time in between taking sips. I'm sure I haven't left anything out, but my legs tremble, and I have to lean my elbows on my knees to stop them jittering. Tea sloshes, dives out of the cup, and lands on my skin. I pretend I haven't noticed.

It dribbles down my bare shin.

"Do you want a cloth for that?" Collier asks, her eyebrows turning into one long strip.

They need plucking.

"What?" I glance down. "Oh."

Collier cocks her head, and a strange expression flits over her face, then it's gone before I can catch on to what it signified.

"I think we'll leave you to go back to bed, Miss Ordsall." She rises, as does Mr Hanks.

I've messed this up, have come across as some airhead, nothing like when I met them earlier, when I was moody but confident — moody because I don't want my life ruined by what's happened. Not when I'm so happy with my lot. "Sorry. I really am out of it. A double shift, plus staying on longer after what went on . . ."

"You've had quite a few hours awake, then. No wonder you're spaced out." Collier smiles. "I'd be the same. Right, we're off. If you could just quickly read your statement, then sign it at the bottom there . . ."

I take the form from Mr Hanks, the words swimming in front of me, blurry and jumbled. I put my cup down and sign anyway, desperate to crawl back into bed, to get these two out of here so I can forget everything for a while.

They leave, and I return to the bedroom, settling down and closing my eyes. Just as I'm dropping off, a distant, frantic knocking pulls me back, and I open my eyes as though that will help me hear better.

There it is again, that knocking.

What the fuck *is* it?

Then it stops, and I shrug, finally losing myself to sleep.

CHAPTER TEN

Six Months Ago

He stands there staring at himself in the full-length mirror, disbelieving his eyes. Is that really him? Is he there again, right there, in those brown trousers and a white shirt, a taupe tie knotted tight? His hair is a different colour to what he's used to, and it takes a moment to register that he isn't the same anymore — he doesn't look the same as he has for the past ten years.

Things came to a head recently, sending him back there, his past bustling in, taking over the rational side of him, changing him back to the surly person he used to be. Someone who'd grown bitter from a life spent with his mother.

Once she'd died, for a while he'd been content as the recent part of himself — the part he'd suppressed because his mother hadn't liked it. With her gone, it had seemed everything horrible regarding that bitch of a woman had died with her. He'd lived like everyone else, smiling, happy, a great weight lifted, being who he really was inside.

Then someone had activated a memory — someone called Mrs Roberts — and things had gone to shit.

Now he can't stop thinking about her, that lady who had caused so much aggro in his childhood. She had been a player around the time he'd been born, and he'd grown up listening to his mother spouting vitriolic words about her.

And there they had resided in his head, a silent partner, pretending to fade but coming back as soon as a trigger had released them.

A plan had formed, of how he'd get rid of her, because, as his mother had once said: Things would be okay if Mrs Roberts didn't exist.

He'd pushed that woman to the back of his mind when his mother had died, and now look what had happened. Mrs Roberts was back in the forefront, in his actual life, there every work day, babbling on and on, rasping on his nerves.

If she was no longer in the picture, life would go back to how it had been the last ten years — calm, safe, a wonder. He'd be happy again if he was the person he'd become before she had swanned into the care home.

But right now, seeing himself as he used to be, wearing clothes he hasn't worn in so long, has him wanting to cry.

He crumples into a ball on the floor, lying on his side, hugging his legs, knees touching his chin, turning his back to the mirror so he can't see his old self. He'd come so far, only for it to be snatched away from him. His life isn't going to be the same anymore, not until he can get rid of that woman.

It'll take planning, but that's okay. He'd planned for his mother's departure, and that had turned out all right, hadn't it?

Eyes closed, he runs through what he has to do, thinking that even if it takes months, so long as he achieves his objective, things will be fine. Then he won't have to be this side of him, in the brown trousers and the white shirt. In the taupe tie he wants to strangle someone with.

* * *

The Past

He waits in the driver's seat of the taxi — a vehicle he uses to cruise. Sometimes people flag him down, thinking he's a real taxi driver, and he even gives them a ride and pockets the fare. He's done this before — this, this . . . kind of thing — after his mother had told him one particular story about Mrs Roberts and what she'd been before she'd become Mrs Roberts.

It had stuck in his mind, mainly because his father had used Mrs Roberts' services, ruining the trust his mother had in him. Ruining their lives. Leaving them when his mother became 'too unbearable to live with'.

He hates his father for that.

He'd gone out after he'd been told about the 'shenanigans', as his mother had put it, into the night, choosing someone who'd resembled Mrs Roberts and taking her home to his mother.

She'd kicked seven bells of shit out of the lookalike, and he'd finished her off for good. Then he'd dragged her into the basement and practised on her what he wanted to do to his mother at some point in the future.

Now, while he waits for an appropriate person to appear, he drums his fingers on the steering wheel, memories crowding in until he can't draw a proper breath. He's suffocating in the misery of what has gone before, drowning even, desperate to be normal but knowing he never will be. Not until his mother and the real Mrs Roberts are dealt with.

Ah, the Right One strolls by, her dark hair long, her legs slim, a short skirt leaving nothing to the imagination. He pretends to be his father for a few seconds, waiting in the car just like he did, picking up Mrs Roberts, who wasn't Mrs Roberts until a few years later. Miss Irene Nicholls, she was. How had his father felt, eyeing her up, knowing what he wanted to do with her? To her?

Rage builds and swamps his body, but finally he can breathe again, his chest rising and falling rapidly, his lungs burning as much as his cheeks.

He starts the taxi and kerb-crawls, pausing right beside her.

Unwinding the window, he stares out at her standing there on the pavement, leaning down to speak to him with her blue eyeshadow and pale-pink lips screaming she's a dirty girl, her fake, black leather jacket a strange brown colour on one shoulder where the amber streetlight splashes its glow.

He jerks his head, hoping she gets the hint, then he drives away, turning left and waiting in a lane that has no lighting, no houses, no nothing. Gaze fixed on the rearview mirror, he waits.

She appears, sauntering along, and he stares out of the open window until she's there.

"Need a taxi?" he asks.

She grins, as though he's said something extremely funny — as though it's some kind of code for 'I need a fuck'.

He doesn't, and he won't touch her like that, but she isn't to know, is she.

She waltzes around the bonnet and opens the passenger-side door, and he tells her to get in the back. Doing as she's told, she shuts the door then slides in behind him.

"Lie down," he says.

She giggles. "This is a different way of going about things. Men usually drive away from here to a safer place — unless you're planning to do me in the lane."

"No, I'm not. And your type can't be seen in my car."

"Ah. Get in trouble at work, will you?"

"Something like that."

He pulls away from the kerb and travels here and there for a few minutes, just to get the taxi seen in several different locations around the time she got in. He's not stupid, he knows what to do, and then he's on his way home, to the place where he grew up, the whole house belonging to him, left to him in his mother's will.

She at least had the decency to do that.

The streetlamp closest to his home isn't lit — 'someone' climbed up the pole and broke the bulb, but he doesn't want to think about who that was now, otherwise it means admitting to the truth: that it was him and he'd planned this. Again.

He doesn't like that side of himself, this side of himself, the man he becomes when anger takes control, when what he's endured staggers back into his head and screws everything up.

He guides her up the path and into the house — the neighbours' lights are off either side, all the way up and down the street.

Locking the door, he waits for her to take her shoes off.

She doesn't.

He's not sure what to do. His mother had always insisted guests removed their footwear.

But his mother isn't here anymore . . .

"Cor," she says, gawping around, bringing him back to the present. "It's not often I get to work in a house. If you pay me two hundred, I'll stay the night."

She'll be staying anyway, and no money will exchange hands.

She moves to mount the stairs, but he shakes his head.

"My bedroom is downstairs," he says, leading the way, the clip-clopping of her heels behind him, each beat drumming it into his head that his mother will be turning in her grave — if she had one — because the shoes might dent the wooden flooring.

He descends into his 'bedroom' — a lie — leaving the light off. Once she's down there with him, he runs back up to secure the door, then he joins her, knowing exactly where he is by instinct. He flicks a wall switch, and the room floods with brightness. She blinks, adjusting her sight he imagines, and looks around, her eyes widening at what she's spotted.

And then she screams.

* * *

A woman whimpers in the corner, naked, her mouth gagged, wrists and ankles tied. She's his pet, a replica of a young Mrs Roberts, and he keeps her drugged during the day and feeds her as little as possible, enough to keep her alive, but he bets her stomach growls most of the time, screaming out for food, and he bets she growls, too, when she's lucid.

She's not at the moment. Her head rests on her shoulder, and she snores. He probably gave her a bit too much medicine earlier. He keeps her so he can watch her suffer like his mother wanted Mrs Roberts to suffer. He sits and watches her sometimes, just stares and stares until his eyes go glassy and out of focus, pleased she's unhappy, bearing the sins of a woman she doesn't even know because his mind won't allow anything different. His mother wouldn't allow it if she were alive either. He knows he's been conditioned, fed tales of woe and anguish, and it had burrowed into his head as he'd grown up, and now it's here to stay. If he makes the scraggy cow in the corner wish for death, to be sorry — really sorry — it'll make everything all right again.

He sets about doing what has to be done.

His mother stands in the other corner, watching him work, as does another lookalike Mrs Roberts, his first attempt at ridding the world of dirty girls. The pair of them don't appear quite as they had in life, but he doesn't mind. Their flaws only show him how he's grown since he'd first practised on them.

With this new dirty girl, his pet, he has a better idea of what works and what doesn't. She won't have wonky eyes or limp fingers like the other two, and he'll tan her skin properly, using a better method. He'll do it the old-fashioned way this time.

He works for ages. That skin of hers is on a tarp in the middle of the floor, and he's using a fleshing knife to scrape away all the fat. Once that's done, along with shaving off her hair, he'll wash her then hang her up to dry on a rack for a few days.

She looks like a human rug minus the fluff, displayed like that.

* * *

A week passes, and it's time to boil her brain until it breaks down into soup. He blends it, creating a paste, and that's enough to rub all over her skin to tan it. He doesn't like the smell and gags, pausing to take deep breaths and force himself not to concentrate on the stench.

Next comes the stretching then the smoking. He drapes her over a tepee-like structure out in the garden in the dark, early hours of the morning, lighting a fire.

And then she's ready.

The wooden mannequin has a moveable head, arms, and legs, and is a similar size to her. He dresses it with her skin. This is his favourite part, where he sews her back together over the body beneath and recreates her, only this time she can't speak, can't move — unless he makes her.

The pet in the corner cries quietly, and it interrupts his calm state. He stops what he's doing and stalks over there, stabbing her a few times with his sewing needle until pinpricks sprout up all over her face. They bleed, and that blood dribbles. Red tears.

She shuts up.

He moves back to his new mannequin. Glass eyeballs and a wig complete the job, and she stares at him somewhat vacantly, as though she doesn't understand why she's there.

She's there because she looks like Mrs Roberts, that's all.

No other reason.

CHAPTER ELEVEN

Close to five o'clock, the shift almost over, Tracy sighed and addressed her team in the incident room. "This is proving to be a bit of a ball ache. No bloody leads from our end — mine and Damon's, I mean. What about you guys?" She'd asked the question of them all but looked at Nada.

Nada sat straighter and swiped up a page of notes. "I rang Gilbert to ask if I could go to view Mrs Roberts' body, but he was busy and said to go there tomorrow. The man who runs Shop on the Go isn't in the frame. He had an accident in his van yesterday and is in hospital with a broken leg. Irene Roberts wasn't on any social media sites. She kept herself to herself when she lived in her former place of residence, except for speaking to her next-door neighbour — a Michelle Armitage. According to Michelle, Irene tended to stay indoors and used to say things like, 'They're coming to get me, so I can't go out.' Sounds a bit weird to me, but the neighbour had no idea what she meant."

Tracy's interest piqued. "So this could mean that whoever 'they' are actually went to 'get' her at the care home and abducted her then killed her." She frowned hard. "But why the hell would anyone want to 'get' her? She was an old woman, for God's sake." She thought back to what

Mr Roberts had said. "This is interesting. Her son told me that for as long as he can remember, his mum had been anxious. Always looked on the dark side, thought if she went out something bad would happen. I took it as anxiety — a lot of people feel like this and think that sort of thing. But *this*? Sounds to me like she had a massive reason to behave the way she did."

"That changes things a bit then, boss," Nada said. "When Tim and Erica came back from interviewing the day staff, they got on with looking into Irene's past — *before* she got married. Want to fill us in?" She glanced at Tim.

He nodded and read from his computer monitor. "She was formally Irene Nicholls. She's got priors in that name but none as Roberts."

Tracy's spine stiffened. "Oh right. What kind of priors?"

"Soliciting." Tim winced.

"You bloody what?"

"I know. She was a regular sex worker by all accounts. Got hauled in a few times for it." Tim counted the lines of text on the screen by tapping the end of his pen on them. "Twenty-eight to be exact."

"Bloody hell, she didn't learn after the first few times of being nicked then, did she." Tracy shook her head. "This alters things dramatically. Fuck, we could be looking at several hundred people — more even — who might have wanted to kill her. Punters, their wives . . . And how long ago was this?"

Erica wrapped a strand of hair around and around her finger. "In the sixties and seventies, boss. She got married in seventy-three, had her son two months later."

"Oh heck, so he could belong to anyone," Tracy said. "Frankie Roberts might not be her husband's."

Damon shook his head as though she'd said something out of turn.

"What? It's true." Tracy wagged her finger. "You know as well as I do there's nowt queer as folk. Look at the last big case. One bloke getting three women pregnant. They all hid the secret so well — who's to say this family doesn't have similar stuffed up their sleeves?"

"Fair point." Damon shrugged. "So do you think her son knows and is covering up?"

"No. Unless he's a sodding good actor. He seemed as puzzled about it as we are. But you can bet someone made good on their promise — because from what Irene said to her neighbour, she knew someone was out to get her, just didn't know when." Tracy rubbed her temple. "Imagine that, living in fear all your life, then as time goes by, you tell yourself they're not coming, then when you're old, there they are, killing you."

Everyone stared at her, mouths hanging.

"Sorry, thinking out loud. But that might have been what happened. We just have to work out who it was and why they were after her — why someone had a years' long grudge. And it'd have to be a pretty fucking big grudge for it to last this amount of time, wouldn't it?"

"Depends how deep the hurt goes, boss," Alastair said.

"Oh, hello, you. Yes, trauma can fester." *I should know.* Tracy smiled then turned to Lara. "Did you find anything of significance?"

Lara shook her head. "Afraid not. I looked into Mr Roberts again, just to double-check, and there's nothing more than what we found earlier."

Tracy pursed her lips in thought. "Nada, other than not being able to see Mrs Roberts' body, did you get anything from Gilbert on the phone?"

"Nothing that he hasn't already told you. He hasn't got around to doing her PM yet," she said.

Tracy sighed again. "Well, there's nothing much we can do today now, so we may as well go home. Tomorrow we'll start on the CCTV closest to Blooming Age — no time whatsoever to have got that done today — and we'll have to contact all sex workers who got pulled in around that time and question them to see if they knew Irene." She looked up at the ceiling, then at her team one by one. "A mammoth task, people. Get a good night's sleep so you're alert tomorrow. If you can get to sleep, that is. I'm thinking I'll be awake mulling all this over. What a bloody mess." She slapped her thighs. "See you tomorrow, you lot."

She left the room and strode to Winter's office. She needed to update the chief and let him know what the team had uncovered — and make him aware she might not be available in the next few days while they sought out this killer, who hopefully wouldn't strike again if he'd only been after Irene.

She tapped on his door and went inside after he'd called, "Enter!"

"Ah, Tracy. Coffee?" He rose and went to his filing cabinet, grabbing the coffee carafe anyway.

"Of course. I tell you, the team love that stuff. Since I ordered that coffee and the machine to go with it and put it in the main office, they've been a lot happier. That vending machine stuff is utter crap."

"You're telling me." He poured two cups. "So, what have you been up to today?"

"A murder, sir."

He paused his pouring and raised his eyebrows. "Didn't have time to let me know earlier or something?"

"No. Sorry, sir. It's been one hell of a day."

He passed her a cup then sat behind his desk. "Start from the beginning. Always the best way." He chuckled.

"Well, what was a murder of an old lady has turned into something far more sinister."

"What can be more sinister than murder?" He blew his drink then sipped.

"Wrong turn of phrase. She was reported missing from the local care home — we weren't aware of that when we went out to see her body. She'd been dumped in a field. Her throat had been slit after death. Anyway, Nada found out about the missing old lady, and we went to the home." She told him about the interviews with the staff at Blooming Age itself then the formal questioning in their homes later.

Then she dropped the bombshell about Irene's anxiety and her previous profession.

"I can see now why you didn't have time to check in with me. Do you need more hands on deck?"

She told him what was on the work menu for tomorrow. "So if we're overwhelmed, yes, but I think the team I've already got are adequate now Alastair is a permanent fixture."

"That took some persuading to get him for you full time, I can tell you," Winter said. "The higher-ups seem to think skeleton crews can manage perfectly well. I reminded them this is a serious crimes squad, nothing like the team Kane ran when he was here."

Tracy's hackles went up, and she drank some coffee to stop herself from saying something she shouldn't.

"You know," Winter said, "I worked the beat back in the seventies when I first started in the force. An old memory has just piped up. I'm sure there was a case back then of a prostitute being attacked by some woman who threatened her life. I'll look into that right now, otherwise it's going to niggle at me if I leave it until the morning. Of course, it could be someone else entirely . . ." He got up and walked to his filing cabinet, opened a drawer, then rummaged around for a while, bringing out a leather diary. The wide spine was cracked, and the corners had worn, showing the beige cardboard beneath. "These books" — he gestured to the drawer — "are my whole time as a police officer. Years of them in there. I kept records so I'd have something to look back on during retirement. Something to be proud of. I didn't realise I'd read them before I left this job — too many times to count, hence me recalling this particular case involving a sex worker."

Tracy couldn't get over it, how he'd kept personal archives like that. "Blimey, sir."

"This is the seventies." He waved the book then sat in his seat again. "If it happened, it'll be in here, on the vice page." He flicked through, found the section, then ran his finger down the page. He did this several times on different pages, then lifted his head to beam at her. "There we go. Irene Nicholls, attacked by a supposedly unknown woman."

"Why supposedly?"

"Because I recall it distinctly now. She had a shifty look in her eye when I asked her if she knew who had given her a beating. If I remember rightly, she didn't want it followed up."

"Hmm. So maybe this attacker is the one we're after now. I have to say, I'm impressed by your memory."

He snapped the book shut. "It helps having these to browse through."

"So you said she didn't want the attack followed up. Does that mean it wouldn't have been in the main log and that's why we didn't get a hit on that incident when the team looked into her past?"

"It would have been logged as something I had attended — it happened in the red-light district, as it was known back then — but as she didn't want her name involved, I probably didn't put it in."

"God. A can of worms or what . . ."

"Indeed. Now, are you going to finish that coffee then get yourself home? After the day you've had, you're going to need all the rest you can get."

Tracy drank the remainder in silence, thinking about the case and what a pickle it was. How the hell did you go about finding an unknown assailant from forty-odd years ago?

She pushed out of her seat, put the cup on the filing cabinet, then smiled at Winter. "Wish me luck, sir, because it looks like I'm going to bloody need it."

"Sleep on it and come in tomorrow raring to go."

"I don't know about raring, sir, but I'll give it my best."

CHAPTER TWELVE

Tracy joined Damon in the incident room. "Anything else come up while I was gone?" She half hoped there would be so they could catch this sick bastard sooner rather than later, but at the same time, she'd had enough and needed her home comforts. Nothing like your arse stuck to your sofa, drink in hand, and the TV on to make all life's ills disappear for a while, was there?

"Nope." Damon smiled. "Want me to cook tonight?"

She shook her head, not wanting to wait as long as it took for him cook from scratch. While his meals were lovely, and she was grateful for them, sometimes a bit of junk food was needed to soothe the soul. "I don't know about you, but I fancy one of those fresh pizzas from Morrisons. They only take twenty minutes in the oven, don't they? You up for that?"

"It'll do. Quick and easy. I fancy a beer as well. Let's go the whole hog, eh? Eat and drink unhealthy shit."

Tracy wasn't going to argue with that.

They left the building, and on the way to the supermarket, the hairs on the back of Tracy's neck stood on end. She glanced in the rearview and clocked the number of cars behind her. Three. One red, one blue, one grey. Ford, BMW, and she couldn't make out the last one — too far away.

The driver behind, in the Ford, a bloke in a black jacket, his blond hair cropped short, was basically up her arse, so she tapped the brake pedal a few times in quick succession to warn him to back off.

Twat.

The BMW was farther back, and she could just make out a redheaded woman. The third, no chance of seeing who was inside.

She made it to Morrisons, as did the following vehicles, and she waited in the car after turning the engine off to see who got out of the others. There was the man, running towards the doorway, trying not to get wet from the sudden onslaught of rain that smacked the tarmac so hard it bounced back up again. The BMW woman popped open a brolly then got out — sensible. The grey car Tracy couldn't see.

Shrugging, Tracy decided to park the car closer to the entrance. The rain stopped as abruptly as it had started, and she moved to get out.

"Coming in?" she asked.

"Nah, I'll stay in here, if you don't mind."

She went into the shop, leaving Damon to browse on his phone. She went to the fresh food section and stared at the pizzas on offer. Selecting a meat feast, she then zipped down the alcohol aisle to pick up a bottle of red and a four-pack of Corona. Her ears buzzed inside, as though bugs ferreted about in them, and, uneasy, she turned her head to check her surroundings.

People shopped as usual, taking no notice of her whatsoever. A toddler stared her way and poked his tongue out. Tracy returned the gesture, and the child wailed.

Quickly, Tracy went to the till and waited in the queue, thinking of Colin Spinks, a victim in a previous case, and how he'd stood in an Asda queue holding a bag of Pampers for his baby daughter, not knowing he wouldn't make it home.

She shivered.

Life was so damn unpredictable, wasn't it?

With two people in front of her, she had time to contemplate how people lived such different lives. Some were so lucky not to experience any form of abuse whatsoever, while others, like herself, had it in spades. Did the universe pick certain people to throw shit at or what? Spinks had also been abused — mentally and sometimes physically by his mother, although he hadn't been her biological son. The woman's diary had been filled with what she'd done to him over the years, and it had churned Tracy's stomach, yet oddly, she'd also felt a sliver of pity for her. She'd endured so much, so it wasn't any wonder she'd gone a bit skew-whiff in the head.

The conveyor belt had some space on it now one of the customers had gone, so Tracy grabbed a grocery divider and popped her things down. She stared around the shop to stop herself from thinking too much. The Past wasn't the best place to revisit, and that reminded her to look up a reputable therapist when she got home. It really was time to face a few things. It would be hard, but she'd have to plough through it. Keeping it all locked up inside was asking for trouble. It festered, poisoned her every time a snippet of a memory managed to escape.

She couldn't allow it to go on. It wasn't healthy for her or Damon.

Then it was her turn to be served.

"Need a bag, love?" The cashier whipped Tracy's goods over the barcode reader. The blips indicated she ought to get her card out and pay instead of just standing there, spaced out like Chrissy Ordsall had been.

She hoped the woman had managed to get back to sleep.

"Please," Tracy managed.

"Looks like a nice night in," the cashier said, nodding knowingly at Tracy's purchases and baring her teeth in a disturbing grin — one of those weird characters from horror movies. "Need help with your packing?"

Tracy said please again. She appreciated the blonde woman bagging her things had probably been taught to converse while working, but Tracy wasn't the best person to try that with. Much as she wished she could natter and reveal an insight into her life to a stranger, she couldn't. So she smiled tightly, hovered her card over the machine for a contactless payment, then grabbed her bag and the receipt.

"Have a nice night," the cashier said, her smile somewhat forced this time.

Tracy would bet the woman said something entirely different in her head: *Have the shittiest night ever, you moody bitch.*

Tracy owned that title already and had the crown that went with it.

She wore it often.

As she walked past the cigarette counter, her neck hairs bristled again. She frowned and cast her gaze about, taking in forty or so things at once, as she'd been trained to do. Absolutely nothing seemed out of the ordinary.

Until she caught sight of a woman with long purple hair and black-framed glasses.

Tracy's heartbeat accelerated, and she shot over to the magazine rack that stood in front of the fresh sandwiches and chilled drinks. The woman scooted away, eyes wide, towards the greeting cards.

Tracy, not mincing words, said, "Who the fuck *are* you?" and slapped her hand on the creepy fucker's shoulder. "You were behind my car at the police station, too. Turn around. Now."

She did, and Tracy could have died and gone to Hell. It wasn't who she'd suspected it was.

It wasn't Lisa.

"Oh, Jesus, I am *so* sorry," Tracy said, removing her hand. "I'm a police officer, and I thought you were someone else."

The woman's eyes watered, and her face flushed bright red. "It's . . . it's okay."

That stammer would haunt Tracy for a while yet.

Shit.

She shook her head as if to show the poor love she really was apologetic, then left the shop, her cheeks hot, nerves pinging. It was no good. She was going to have to stop this malarkey, thinking Lisa was hanging about at every turn. If she spoke to her again, she'd just have to reinforce what she'd told her before.

Fuck off and don't come back — or else.

It was the 'or else' bit that prevented Tracy from hauling Lisa in, proving her sister had killed so she could put her away for a long time. It didn't matter that she'd probably get away with all the murders she'd committed — the ones to do with their insane father, anyway, because Tracy had planted seeds that it had been him who had carried them all out — but there had been a witness to Lisa's latest one. She'd gutted someone in the recent big case, and she could go down for that, no problem. Lisa had left her scarf at the crime scene — *the stupid, thick cow* — and there would be DNA on it that would see her locked behind bars, as well as her link to Tracy.

But Tracy wasn't ready for the inevitable crap Lisa's arrest would bring. Lisa had threatened to open her mouth about everything, and if she finally did, Damon would then know Tracy had been lying to him for God knew how long.

No, the 'or else' wasn't an option. Not if it meant losing him.

She got in the car, wiping all those terrible thoughts from her mind, and leant across to rest her head on Damon's shoulder.

"Bloody love you," she said.

"Blimey. What brought that on?" He put his phone in the centre console.

"Just felt like saying it." She smiled and started the engine, berating herself for fibbing yet again. Would that ever stop?

She doubted it.

When she pulled out of the car park entrance, she glanced in the rearview mirror. The grey vehicle was right up behind her, and the driver was a woman.

Purple hair. Black glasses. Not the same one as in Morrisons, but a woman Tracy knew only too well.

Fuck. I knew she was around.

Tracy shot out onto the road between two cars, got honked at, put her foot down, and checked the mirror again.

Lisa had been prevented from exiting because of traffic snailing it past her front bumper.

Good. It meant that particular worry could be ignored for a while longer.

"Bloody hell, hold your horses," Damon said. "What's the rush?"

"Really hungry," Tracy said, taking a corner at speed.

"Better to get there in one piece, though, eh?"

She lifted her foot a bit and glanced across at him. He frowned at her. She faced the road and continued on.

"I got a meat feast." Was that really all she could think of to say? Yes, because saying anything else regarding her exit from the car park could lead to a conversation that might put her in scalding water.

"Lovely. Looking forward to it. Glad to see you've slowed down," he said.

"What do you make of today?" It was a safer topic. Tepid water. She could handle that.

"It's all a bit of a mess at the moment. Here's hoping we'll discover more tomorrow. It feels a bit wrong not to still be working. I mean, there's a killer out there."

"But most likely a one-off, going by what we've found out so far. Someone was after Irene Roberts and no one else. We can't do a damn thing while running on fumes, you know that."

"Hmm." He sniffed. "Still feels wrong, though."

"That's not like you. What's up?"

"I don't know. Granted, I'm usually all for getting rest and looking at it the next day with fresh eyes, and I'm a fan of not taking work home with us, even though that's difficult sometimes, but this case . . . I don't know. I think it's bothering me because she was old. Like a kid case would get to me more, know what I mean?"

She did. All murders were horrific to deal with, but there was something about the more vulnerable in society that gave their deaths a sadder feel. It shouldn't be that way, but it was.

"We'll find out soon enough." Taking his comment about not bringing work home with them into consideration, she said, "What do you fancy watching on telly tonight?"

"No idea. We'll pick something later."

They arrived, and once inside, Tracy bunged the pizza in the oven and uncorked the red wine. Slouched upstairs to take off her work clothes and grab a quick shower. She dried herself in the bedroom, and her phone went off with a message tone.

"Oh, for fuck's sake."

She sat on the bed, accessed the text, and read:

THAT'S THE SECOND TIME I'VE TRIED TO TALK TO YOU LATELY.

Her stomach bottomed out, and she held a hand to her fast-beating heart. With shaking hands, she tapped out a reply, sick with fear.

WHO IS THIS?

Stupid question. She'd given Lisa her number a while ago. Why hadn't she changed it since? She waited, breath held.

YOU KNOW WHO IT IS.

Tracy whacked out an immediate response.

I'M WARNING YOU, FUCK OFF. I MEAN IT. DON'T CONTACT ME EVER AGAIN. HOW MANY TIMES HAVE I GOT TO TELL YOU THAT?

She closed her eyes and counted to twenty. The text tone went off again, the *ding-dong-ding* abrading her stretched nerves.

I HAVE SOMETHING TO TELL YOU. I WANT TO REPORT A CRIME.

Tracy laughed at that, albeit quietly. Lisa was something else. Just where did she get off doing shit like this? She plugged in her answer.

THEN CONTACT SOMEONE ELSE. I CAN'T HELP YOU. AND WHEN YOU REPORT IT, DO NOT,

AND I BLOODY MEAN THIS, DO NOT TELL THEM YOU ARE MY SISTER OR THAT I KNOW YOU.

She blew out a juddering breath, and a terrible thought entered her mind. If she could kill Lisa and get away with it, she would.

Would I, though?

You did it with John . . .

Another message came, wrenching her out of that particular idea, and Tracy steeled herself to see her sister whining, cajoling to get her own way.

OKAY. SEE YOU AROUND . . .

Tracy blinked. That was *it*? No pressure, no manipulation?

"Fuck, she must be in a good mood."

"What was that?" Damon asked, walking in to sit beside her.

She'd been so caught up with Lisa, she hadn't even heard him come up the stairs. Cursing herself, she placed her phone on the bed, screen side to the quilt. The last thing she needed was Damon seeing any message previews if Lisa texted again. He'd see it was an unknown number and question it.

"Oh, I just told myself to get into a good mood," she said. "Can't be pleasant for you, can it, me always being grumpy." And even these types of little lies counted as wrong, something she shouldn't have to do.

And what did it say about her, spewing them out as easily as she did?

Plus, you want to kill your sister.

Piss off.

"Don't be so hard on yourself." Damon shoulder-bumped her. "I happen to like grumpy ladies." He smiled. "Apart from the likes of Mrs Jones. She's another species, she is."

"Tell me if I ever get like her, won't you?"

Damon rose and walked to the door. "Yep. I draw the line at you behaving like that, although I can kind of predict you'll head that way in your old age. I can just see you in an apron like hers and all. All flowery. Very fetching . . ."

She grabbed a pillow and threw it at him, but it missed and thudded into the doorframe. "You'd better hope I don't turn the cold tap on in the sink when you're in that shower, Hanks."

"You wouldn't dare," he called from the bathroom.

"Try me."

"No, you're all right. I prefer my showers hot."

She smiled, and it faltered when she read through her conversation with Lisa.

Tracy was living on a knife edge. It wasn't that much different to her childhood, really. Events were out of control because of a family member once again.

Would her nightmare ever end?

She deleted all the messages then got dressed, thinking of how she wished she'd looked at Lisa's licence plate so she could run a check on it to see if she'd stolen yet another car. She hadn't even registered what make the vehicle was.

She couldn't think about that now. It was time to switch into one of her other selves, one who didn't have the weight of the world on her shoulders.

There wasn't anything for it except carry on.

But she was used to that.

CHAPTER THIRTEEN

He waits in the dark down the street, the taxi warm, a slight breeze sneaking through the open driver's-side window. They're there at the top of the T-junction, those women, but Dirty Girl isn't. He's tempted to get out and ask some of the others whether the woman he wants will be out tonight at some point, or if she's just with someone else for the moment, but it isn't wise to bring attention to himself in that way. Being out of his car like that . . .

No.

While he observes, he thinks about the task to come, where he has to kill Dirty Girl and skin her, tan her, then make her into a whole new person. A good person. A better one. A woman who can't cause trouble in a marriage and wreck a child's life by her actions because said child's mother lost her fucking mind and expected him to be who he wasn't.

"Here, Wear these." Mother hands him some clothing.

"Why, Mummy?"

"Because I said so."

"But why?"

"Because maybe your father will take more notice of you dressed like that. It's time to change yourself. Be someone he might like. Then he might stick around instead of doing what he does."

"What does he do, Mummy?"

"Never you mind."

He blinks the past away. Thinks about his next steps. He'll add Dirty Girl to the row in the basement, beside the others, and then it will all be over. He can return to how he's been for the past ten years, never wearing these sorts of clothes again or speaking in this voice.

He doesn't like this voice.

He doesn't like it that he's been forced into the person his mother created. He was never that person, not really, but he had to pretend to be. Just like now.

Another unsavoury female arrives, and from here he thinks it might be Dirty Girl. Same hair length, same thin frame, similar clothes to what she had on when he'd taken her to Blooming Age and put her in the old wing.

Could it be her?

He starts the engine and cruises forward, stopping at the end to make sure his eyes haven't deceived him. Sadly, they have. She stands beneath a streetlamp, and it's clear now that it isn't the slut he wants. Still, he can beckon her over and ask a few questions, see if that throws anything up.

He flashes his headlights, and several filthy creatures stare over, some shielding their eyes from the harsh glare. He dips the beams then waves, hoping one of them will walk across to him.

He's in luck.

A black-haired tart approaches, reaching his window and smiling, her teeth stained as though she's on heroin or meth. Or perhaps she eats too much sugar and they've rotted. He doesn't much care. Bad teeth won't stop her from telling him what he wants to know.

She leans her forearms on the door and pokes her head inside. Her breath smells like mint and something he doesn't want to think about. She smiles again, and the closeup of the stumps in her mouth has his stomach rolling over.

He clears his throat. "Is Aurora out tonight?" That's the name Dirty Girl had given him when he'd picked her up last time.

"She isn't, no." She cocks her head, and a lock of hair falls from her shoulder to dangle in front of her.

"Do you know when she'll be out again?" He's not sure what's happening now with his shifts. They've been given the night off, but that doesn't mean they won't have to catch up by working when they usually wouldn't. Zello can be a hard-hearted bitch when she has a mind.

"I don't know." Bad Teeth sighs.

He blinks from the strength of the scent gusting his way and holds back a retch. "I need to see her. It's important. I have a message from her pimp." It's all he can think of to say.

"Oh . . ." She frowns and pulls back, standing upright and wiping her brow, as though what he's said brought on a heavy sweat. "I . . . Oh, Christ. I know where she lives. Will that help?"

"Tell me," he says, his heartrate spiking. *Can it be this easy? Really?*

"I don't know the street name or the number, but I know where it is and would recognise the door if you take me there."

This isn't what he wants, but it might be the only chance he has for a while if Zello makes him work one of his usual nights off. "Get in."

She scoots around the back of the car and plonks herself beside him, closing the door a little too hard.

He doesn't like that.

"You go back down this road, then take a left," she says, stabbing the seat belt connector into the slot.

He reverses all the way, not caring if another car should come along. Then he does a three-point turn at the end and noses up to the intersection. Nothing is coming either way, and he's pleased — he doesn't need anyone clocking his whereabouts at the moment. He takes the left, then she directs him right, then left again.

Dirty Girl's street is a bad one, going by the state of the houses, the bricks all chipped, the gardens overrun with copious amounts of rubbish — fridges, a mattress, and even a bloody Asda shopping trolley.

"Just there," she says, pointing at a house with an outside light on that bleeds yellow beside a scabby green door, the paint peeling, especially around the handle. "I went there once for a threesome. She has a room there. Well, a bedsit really."

He studies the windows, wondering which room Dirty Girl's is or if she even has one at the front. "Go and get her."

Bad Teeth climbs out, huffing, and says, "You're going to pay me for my time, aren't you? I'm losing custom by doing this."

"Yes, yes." He waves her away, thinking twenty quid should do it.

If she wants more, she can whistle for it.

She leaves the car door open, and he's grateful for the cooler air floating in. She walks to the green door, knocking loudly. No lights are on, but that doesn't mean no one's in. Dirty Girl could be at the back of the house. He hopes.

Time passes, in reality only around a minute or so, but to him it seems like an hour. Frustration builds, and he takes a deep breath to steady his anger. He can't bear to look at Bad Teeth standing on the step, knowing what she does for a living. It's creating a maelstrom of unsettled emotions inside him, and memories of the past threaten to crowd his mind. So he glances at the street to check for anyone out and about. It's clear of witnesses, and that soothes him somewhat.

He thinks about seeing Dirty Girl again. Can he control the impulse to kill her immediately, in front of her fellow filthy colleague — if they can be classed as such? Dirty Girl won't recognise him — he doesn't look the same as the times she's already seen him, so he's safe in that she will probably get in his car and drive away with him to make a sale, just like she'd been prepared to walk so far to Blooming Age without querying where they were off to, so eager was she to score some money.

It's the root of all evil, that.

Bad Teeth turns and looks at him, waving to catch his attention. He sighs out a breath of irritation and gestures for her to come back. She returns to the car and gets in.

"She's not there," she says, stating the sodding obvious.

"So I see." What should he do? Sit here all evening until Dirty Girl comes back? Or . . .

He chooses 'or'. It means he can get rid of some tension if he does that.

"Never mind," he says. "Shut the door and buckle up. I'll use you instead."

She smiles at that and does as she's told, and he peels away from the kerb, drawing to the end of the street and taking note of the name of it. The number on the green door — fifty-seven — is imprinted in his brain. He'll never forget where she lives now.

"What do you fancy then?" his passenger asks, twirling her hair around a finger topped with a ragged, bitten nail.

He doesn't fancy anything other than what he has in mind but doesn't want to tell her that. "Just a basic service, that's what I want."

"What, like a blow job or something?"

She'd have a difficult time giving him one of those, but he doesn't tell her that either.

"Or something." He hides a smile.

He heads for home, thinking of how skinning her won't take so long because she's a tiny person. This is pleasing, and he feels a little better than when they'd been outside Dirty Girl's house. The anger is replaced with single-minded determination, him focusing on what he needs to do. He can't have this woman beside him walking around knowing he's looking for Dirty Girl. It'll lead to all sorts of madness if she tells anyone and says he drives a taxi. It wouldn't be long then before the police came knocking at his door when it's discovered Dirty Girl is missing.

Because she *will* be at some point.

"Where are you taking me?" Bad Teeth asks.

"My house."

"Oh." She moves her hand to undo her seat belt but leaves it secured. "I don't do houses. Sorry. Can you drop me off here? And you still owe me for losing money going to Aurora's, remember."

"I'll drop you off up here then," he says, abandoning plan A and moving to B, driving towards the abandoned warehouses behind the town centre shops. If she's going to be funny about things, he's better off getting rid of her there.

"Thanks. Fifty quid, right?" She unclips her belt as they approach his destination.

Fifty quid. She's got to be joking.

He doesn't answer, just swerves onto the concrete outside the warehouses and parks in a dark corner. His headlight beams splash on the crumbling bricks. He switches them off.

These days, the warehouse windows are boarded up. A while ago, they had been left as open spaces, no glass, and the homeless dossed down inside. No one should be around now their former digs are unavailable, so he'll be safe to do what he fancies.

There's an alley that leads to the town, and Clarks' shoe shop is to one side. He hates Clarks shoes. None of his friends had them when he'd been at school, and they'd taken the piss that his mother had bought them for him. They were ugly and clunky, terribly out of fashion back then, and the reminder of that shop grates on his nerves.

That's all right. It'll fuel the fire burning a hole in his gut.

He gets out of the car at the same time she does and makes a show of pulling money out of his trouser pocket. He thumbs through the notes while she advances towards him. With fifty pounds in hand, he holds her payment out. As she reaches to take it, he grips her wrist with his free hand and stuffs the cash away so fast she barely has time to squeal.

He punches her in the face repeatedly until she staggers backwards, her arse hitting the concrete, her torso reclining in slow motion. The thud when her skull connects with the ground sends him to that place where he never wanted to go again, changing him from who he's strived to be the last ten years into something . . . other.

Mrs Roberts has a lot to answer for.

He kicks the prostitute in the head, pain shooting up his big toe, fuck it, and she rolls onto her side, groaning and crying, hands over her ears. He has no sympathy for her. Reaching into his back pocket, he draws his knife out and slits her throat, the skin opening like a goddamn pitta bread, blood surging out, a geyser. Then he pokes her with his foot so she's on her back, and he kneels, hovering his face close to hers so he can watch the life fade from her eyes by the light of his phone screen.

It's beautiful.

Once her soul has gone, he stands and selects his torch app, flashing it over his front to check for blood. For God's sake, he's only just cleaned his other car, and now he'll have to scrub the taxi — blood spatter soaks into his shirt, and he's a fool if he thinks none of it will get on the driver's seat. He steps back, his foot going down into a puddle-filled hole where the council haven't bothered filling the cracks and craters in the old, wrecked car park. The water reaches his ankles.

He lifts his foot then kneels again to wash the knife, his crimson-covered hand, his face, and even though the water's filthy, he doesn't care. He strips his shirt off and plunges it into the puddle until the blood is nothing but a pink stain, then uses the material to wipe his stomach where the red stuff got through.

Home beckons, and he gathers his shirt, phone, and blade then drives away with them on his lap, satisfied with the night's work. He valets the taxi in his garage, and bed is only an hour or so away. He's tired, worn out to his bones from the exertion, the emotion, and he deserves to shut his eyes and wake up tomorrow with only one more job to do.

Find Dirty Girl.

CHAPTER FOURTEEN

Up early after a surprisingly solid night's sleep, Tracy was raring to go. Cracking on with this case was at the forefront of her mind, but she went through the mail in her office to get it out of her way first. CCTV was being checked on the roads that led to the main one outside Blooming Age, and the other tasks they'd discussed last night had been distributed to the team. Everyone had been determined to find this killer quickly when they'd had their briefing at eight this morning.

She finished the mail and quickly typed out what she'd done yesterday so she didn't forget by the time she had to write out her official reports. She should fill them out each evening, but who the fuck had an hour or more spare for that when an investigation was in full swing? Then she bit the bullet and found a therapist in the online version of the *Yellow Pages* before she bottled out. She selected a woman who had several good reviews, one patient raving about how their whole life had changed after just three sessions.

That suited Tracy no end.

She navigated to the therapist's website and found a photograph showing a face belonging to a woman Tracy estimated to be in her mid-forties. Poised, with styled brown hair, there was more of a barrister look about her than anything.

She'd do.

Tracy made the call to book an appointment, her voice trembling, which pissed her off. The receptionist gave her tomorrow at six in the evening. Tracy just hoped she'd get there with such a small margin after her shift finished. She put the phone in the dock, her hand shaking. Eyes closed, she told herself it was the best thing, what she was doing, actively seeking help to end the nightmare her life had been since she was a small kid.

You can do this. You can.

She opened her eyes at a knock on the door. "Come in." Post scooped off the desk and shoved into a drawer, she smiled at Nada. "What can I do for you?"

Nada stood in front of the desk. "In all the faff yesterday when we shared what we'd found out, I forgot to mention where Irene Roberts' old neighbour lives — where Irene used to live before she went to Blooming Age. I wasn't sure if you'd want to go and speak to her yourself or with any other neighbours, because *a certain person* might well know something that will help us . . ."

Tracy narrowed her eyes. "That sounds like you have a big revelation for me."

"You could say that, boss."

"Come on then. Where does she live?"

Nada cringed. "Robin's Way."

"What?" Tracy shook her head. "I had enough of that bloody street from the other case." She sighed. "But, yes, you're right. Mrs Jones — fuck me sideways, really? — will probably have some snippet or other we can use, even though she claimed she isn't nosy. What number are we talking for the other neighbour?"

"Eighty-four."

"Okay. I suppose that can be the first stop for me and Damon today. He *will* be pleased . . ." The last was wrapped up in sarcasm with a shiny bow of derision. He *wouldn't* be too chuffed, but if going to see the old Jones bitch meant getting information, they'd have to grin and bear it, although grinning was a bit too much to ask. "Right, is that all you wanted to tell me?"

"Yes, boss. Sorry I forgot."

Tracy waved the apology away. "It's fine. If you'd told me last night, I'd have wanted to go around there then, so it's a good job you didn't." On second thought, maybe it would have been better. She wouldn't have seen Lisa. Wouldn't have got those bloody texts. Still, there was nothing she could do about it now. You couldn't change the past.

More's the pity.

"I'll be getting on now then." Nada smiled and left.

Tracy buzzed to Damon's desk phone in the incident room. "Guess where we're going?"

"God. Where?"

"To see our old pal." She fought back a smile.

"We don't have any pals here yet."

She imagined him frowning. "Aww, yes we do. Have you forgotten Hilda?"

"Bloody *Jones*?"

She barked out laughter. "That's the one."

"What do we need to see *her* for? Look, is this one of your rare jokes? Because if it is, it isn't funny."

"Sadly not. Robin's Way — it's where Irene Roberts used to live."

"Blimey. That street . . ."

"I know. So this is your five-minute warning."

"Righty-oh. Shit . . ."

Tracy went for a quick wee, and while washing her hands, she stared at herself in the mirror and again contemplated dying her hair. That brought Lisa to mind. Why the hell she'd gone for purple was anyone's guess. Mind you, it was so different from the black, and with those glasses she'd chosen, it was doubtful Damon would recognise her now. Tracy supposed she should be thankful Lisa had taken her advice on board. At least she'd done as she'd been told that time.

She shook her head to erase her sister from her mind, dried her hands, and met Damon in the incident room. Addressing the team, she said, "Anything to report yet?"

Erica swivelled her chair to face Tracy. "Nothing on CCTV so far. We started earlier in the evening, from six, so there's a fair bit to get through."

"Yeah, my eyes are crossing," Tim said, scratching the back of his ear.

Tracy nodded to acknowledge she'd heard them. "Alastair, anything from you, or are you still nursing a sore head?"

He cleared his throat and blushed as everyone roared. "Nothing yet, boss. And my head's much better, thank you for asking."

Tracy grinned. "Lara?"

"I'm going through the old records again, checking every entry in the seventies regarding sex workers, then I'm passing the names on to Nada."

"Okay, thanks. You could ask Winter for some help on that. He's got some logs he kept. Let him know I sent you, all right?"

Lara nodded.

"So, Nada, you'll be trying to chase these women up, yes?" Tracy cocked her head.

"Yes, boss. I'll be following up marriage records and the like to see if they're known by different names now. Damon was helping me with that — you found a couple of them already, didn't you?" she said to him.

"Yes," he said. "The info's on my desk."

"I'll take over contacting them, shall I?" Nada asked.

"If you would for now, thanks. We're off to speak to Hilda Jones." Tracy grimaced.

"Not that nasty one we dealt with before, surely?" Tim asked.

"The very same, so wish us luck." Tracy walked to the door. "Keep up the good work, guys. I appreciate you all." She was greeted with a few shocked expressions — she rarely gave praise. Wouldn't want them thinking she was a pushover.

Down the stairs she went, and once outside, she strode to her car and waited for Damon inside. He got in, and they were off to Robin's Way.

"I made an appointment," she said.

"Good."

How was it he knew exactly what she was talking about? In tune or what?

"How do you feel about that?" he asked.

"Is that question meant to be funny?"

"What do you mean?"

"Well, that's what therapists say, isn't it? 'And how do you *feel* about that?' in a droning, patronising voice."

"Shit. I didn't mean it like that. Please don't get into one of your snits over it."

"I'll try not to." *God, I'm such a cow.* She opted for a different subject. "Are you handling Jones, or shall I?"

"You have a go first. If she's in her usual mood and winds you up, I'll take over."

"Maybe she won't be so belligerent now her son's dead."

"Tracy . . . That was a bit insensitive, love."

She bit her tongue before she put her leg in her mouth, let alone her foot. "Sorry, but she gets on my wick. I'll attempt to be professional with her, okay? But you know how it goes with that woman, so I can't promise anything."

"Yeah, best not to promise. You usually break them — on purpose, you sod."

She laughed.

"So," he said, "we're going to see her to find out if she knew Irene Roberts?"

"Yes. Might as well go and visit Irene's old neighbour while we're at it. Number eighty-four. Jones might not know Michelle Armitage — that's what the woman's name is, isn't it? — because she lives at the other end of the street, but it's worth a shot."

In Robin's Way, she parked outside Jones' and took a deep breath. They left the car and approached her door, only for it to swing open in true Jones fashion before they'd even had a chance to knock.

"What the hell are *you* doing here?" Jones snapped. "I'm in there making a cup of tea—"she jerked her thumb backwards — "and who do I see but a bad penny — you — and a shiny, welcome pound coin — him. What do you want?" She crossed her arms beneath her huge tits and glared.

"Still the same then, Mrs Jones? Grief obviously hasn't mellowed you," Tracy said. "We're investigating a murder, and we—"

"Bloody hell! Another one? This place has gone to the dogs since you two rolled into town."

"Actually, it was a shithole with a high crime rate before we arrived, so nothing's changed. And, yes, there's been another one, although it hopefully won't be anything to do with you like the last three." It was low of Tracy to get in a second dig like that, but it wasn't like she gave a toss. She gave as good as she got.

"Still spiteful, I see." Jones shook her head in obvious disgust.

"Do you know an Irene Roberts?" Tracy waited for the spiel about Jones not being nosy. It came immediately. Once the woman had finished, Tracy said, "Well?" and resisted tapping her foot.

"I don't know her well. She moved recently. Old people's home, so the word is on the grapevine." She sniffed. "Won't catch me in one of those places."

"Did you ever hear any rumours about Irene?"

"Might have done."

Tracy gritted her teeth. "What did you hear, or are you waiting for me to beg? Because I won't, you know. I'll find out from someone else along here." She indicated the street, raising her hand. "Your call."

Jones pursed her lips and stared up as though thinking. *More like trying to wind me up.*

"Well . . ." Jones lowered her gaze to make eye contact with Tracy. "There was something I heard once, years ago.

When I was in the local little shop, Michelle was talking to the cashier who happens to be her sister."

"And that's Michelle Armitage, I take it."

Jones looked as though her ego bubble had been burst. She must have thought Tracy didn't know who Michelle was.

"Yes, as it happens," Jones huffed. "Michelle was saying something about people being after Irene. You know, *after* her, and not in a good way either."

"I know that already, yes. Anything else?"

"Well, if you know, what are you asking me for?"

"In case you had any other information."

"No. Like I said, I'm not nosy."

"Of course you aren't." Tracy bit back a nasty retort. "Well, thank you for your time."

"'Ere, don't you go walking off without telling me who's been bumped off. And none of this 'We're not at liberty to say' rubbish like they use on my soaps either."

"We're not at liberty to say, Mrs Jones, sorry." *Sorry my arse.*

Tracy led the way down the path, Damon tailing her, and they walked side by side towards Armitage's in silence until Jones was out of earshot.

"You did well, considering," Damon said.

"I wanted to rip her bloody head off."

"I know. Glad you didn't. Can't be doing with you being had up for murder."

Tracy's stomach clenched, and a cold sweat broke out all over. She swallowed, her throat dry, and couldn't risk glancing at him for fear he'd see the truth in her eyes. It had just been a comment, something anyone might say, but it had hit too close to home.

"Can't be doing with it myself. That's why I didn't go for her. Here we are, look." She gestured to a gravel path that led to a pristine white UPVC door. She walked up to it and pressed the bell button.

The door opened a smidgen, and Tracy brought out her ID at the same time as Damon. They showed the woman, only a slice of her visible through the three-inch gap. One blue eye, no nose, a ruddy cheek, one half of bright-red lips, and a cloud of wispy white hair.

"Michelle Armitage? DI Tracy Collier and DS Damon Hanks. We're here to talk about Irene."

"Oh." She widened the gap and stepped back. Slight of frame, she looked like a gentle breeze would knock her over. "Better come in then."

They went inside and waited while Armitage closed the door. She shuffled into the living room, Tracy and Damon following. Damon got out his notebook, and after Armitage offered them a seat, they sat on the sofa while the woman took a pine wooden rocking chair with a pink paisley cushion on it.

"We know about what you told our colleague, Michelle, and we just wanted to see if you'd remembered anything else."

Armitage rocked, gripping the polished armrests. "I have, as it happens. Funny how that goes. You think you've recalled everything, then in the middle of the night, when you're staring at the ceiling, something else pops up."

Tracy smiled. "Can you tell me what it is?"

"Well, shortly after Irene had told me the other thing — you know, about people coming to get her — she said something that struck me as odd. She was poorly with the flu, and I'd gone round there with some over-the-counter medication for her as she didn't like to leave the house if she could help it. Her son was away on holiday with his family at the time, see, so he couldn't get them for her like he usually does. Anyway, I had a key to hers, so I let myself in, and she was on the sofa under a blanket. She had her eyes closed, and she said, all delirious like, 'Is that you? Have you found me, Carol?' Well, as far as I knew, Irene didn't know any Carol."

"So that was odd?" Tracy didn't see it that way. People had lives before they met certain people, and she could have known this Carol before she became friends with Armitage.

"No, the next bit was odd. She said something like, 'I'm a wicked woman, doing what I did, so if you're here for me,

I understand.' Then she said, 'I'm so sorry your husband left you because of me.' You can imagine what went through my mind, can't you? That Irene had an affair with someone. But it didn't seem to ring true. Irene wasn't that type of woman."

Oh, she was, except what she did wasn't affairs as far as we know.

"Anything else?" Tracy asked.

"No. But if I think of something more, I'll give that nice lady a ring, the one I spoke to before."

Tracy could have been affronted at that. She wasn't. Not many people would choose to speak to her if they could help it. She wouldn't speak to herself in someone else's position either. "All right, that would be a big help. Thank you."

Her phone trilled, and she glanced at Damon, telling him with her eyes to wrap the interview up while she took the call outside. On the pavement, she answered without looking at the screen.

"Hello, DI Collier."

"It's me, boss."

Vic Atkins, the daytime desk sergeant.

"Oh fuck . . ." she said.

"You got that right. There's been another murder."

CHAPTER FIFTEEN

A swarm of SOCOs took pictures of the car park outside the warehouses, searched for evidence, and placed markers every time they found something. Tracy stood beside Gilbert in a marquee, dressed in the required whites, Damon off somewhere behind her, probably so he could turn away and leg it out without them seeing once the body was revealed.

"These bloody buildings ought to either be torn down or revamped." Gilbert shook his head. "They're an eyesore as they are, a waste, not to mention this is the ideal spot to do things like this." He flapped his gloved hand at the sheet-covered body. "No one comes down that alley at night unless they're up to no good, and most people wouldn't visit here via the road when there's nothing but the warehouses and that old office block."

Tracy glanced over at the offices. A man had run his accountancy firm from one of them back in the day, had sex with two of his secretaries, raped a third, and ended up being a father to three kids who'd then got murdered one by one recently. That case would live inside Tracy forever. It was her first in this town, her first as the lead detective of the serious crimes squad that had been set up as lawbreaking had skyrocketed around these parts.

"I have to agree," she said. "This place is basically asking for people to come here to do bad things. Drug handovers, the sex workers on the other side of the road from the alley doing business—" A thought cut off her words. Was that the patch Lisa worked, just a few feet away? Or did she frequent the other one?

Dare I go out there one night and see?

No. Don't.

"Hmm." Gilbert crouched. "Best you have a look, make your own mind up about what you'll see — what I mean by that is: who did it."

"That doesn't sound good." She didn't go down on her haunches, preferring to stand.

"Are you ready?"

She nodded.

He pulled the sheet back. Female. Long black hair. Slender, and with a neck that gaped open, dark-gold fat globules at the edges, almost dried out, like crystallised pus, what with the heat of the night and this morning. Last evening's downpour had done nothing but ramp up the humidity. The weather was far too hot, even for summer — the UK wasn't supposed to be like the fucking Med, was it?

Those who said global warming wasn't real were in denial.

"Um . . . okay." Tracy took a deep breath.

She looks like Lisa . . .

The method of murder was obvious. She recalled Gilbert's lesson about blood — this woman had had her throat slit while she'd been alive. Crimson coated her clothing, her face, where it had perhaps shot upwards from her heart pumping away, and landed on her skin, an obscene version of a red paint splash. A whole can of it.

"Bloody hell," Tracy said.

"That's one way of putting it. *Bloody* hell. Get it?"

"That was lame for you," she said.

Gilbert grinned and pointed to the victim's neck. "See that slit there?"

"Christ, how can I not?"

"Well, that was a right-handed person going from the victim's right to her left. The slice starts shallow, then goes deeper, so more force at the middle and tail end of it. This also suggests to me she wasn't in this position — on her back — when the slice occurred. She was more likely on her left side. Harder to get good purchase that way, which further corroborates my theory about the shallow end."

"But what about her facial injuries?" she asked.

There were many. Bruised eyes, both of them swollen so it appeared she had boiled eggs beneath her skin with a black line down the middle of each. Her nose looked broken, skewing off to the side. And her lips — Christ. Split in two places on the top one, the lower reminding Tracy of Botox injections gone wrong.

"Someone kicked her head in," Gilbert said. "An angry someone. What do you think about who did it?"

Tracy shrugged. "I'm inclined to say it was a boyfriend or an ex with a bone to pick. Maybe she pissed him off."

"Pissed him off quite a bit, going by this. Maybe she didn't cook his dinner just right — and I'm not making a joke there. It doesn't take much to tip some people over the edge."

"Sadly, no, it doesn't. Or it could be a random attack — I say that because of the location. Given that just down the alley is a pick-up spot for sex workers . . . you can see where I'm going with that." She peered at the face closely, unable to tell if it was Lisa because it was in such a mess. Would it bother her if it *was* her? She allowed herself a second or two to think about that and came up with an answer she didn't much like. She'd be relieved she wouldn't have to tell any more lies if this was her sister. She could let go of John's murder — Lisa would well and truly go to her grave with that particular death laid solely at her feet. "But I have a feeling you're going to squash that and tell me something I don't want to know."

Gilbert stood, his knees or some other joint of his clicking. "I might be wrong, but I'd say the same knife was used on Mrs Roberts."

Although she'd kind of been expecting that, Tracy still internally said *what*? "How the hell do you know that?"

"Look at the beginning of the slice. It's got the same strange curl to it as Mrs Roberts. Maybe the blade is bent on the end, or the killer has a signature flick, as it were, a way he slices."

"Okay . . . So now I have to work out why these two women's deaths are related. An old lady and a young one. Both sex workers — all right, Irene gave it up years ago, but still. And I assume this one's young. Can't really tell, can we?"

"I can by the skin." He moved the woman's top, stiff with dried blood. It was more like he lifted a sheet of cardboard. "See? Young skin. Twenties, I'd say, maybe closing in on thirty."

Her stomach was pink from where the blood had soaked through, but no, this wasn't an older woman. Her belly was flat, as though she hadn't eaten an awful lot in her life — or she'd worked out, so no flab had had time to form.

"This doesn't look like the stomach of someone who's had kids," she said, thinking of her own belly.

"Oh, you'd be surprised. Some women don't get stretchmarks, and their tummies go down nicely as though they'd never had a baby in there."

"Interesting. So, considering what I've found out so far . . ." Tracy bit her lip. "I've got someone 'coming to get' Mrs Roberts — and they did. I'm now wondering whether this is some kind of network this lady here was a part of. You know, an organised gang that goes about targeting people for a price? I'm thinking that because a neighbour of Mrs Roberts said she was convinced someone was after her — after Mrs Roberts. Had this lady here outlived her usefulness? She knew too much so had to be silenced? So many possibilities, and I'm letting my imagination take over."

"I don't envy you working this out." Gilbert grimaced.

"I don't envy *you*," she said, thinking of him having to cut up this victim to find out whatever he could to help Tracy.

"I've told you before. Justice spurs me on. They deserve it." He gazed at the body, his mouth downturned, eyebrows pulled together. "So much hate with this one. Makes you wonder why a person feels such a high degree of it — enough to kill someone."

"I've found people's pasts have a lot to do with it." *Don't they just.* "Some have endured so much, and sometimes, there comes a point where they can't take anymore, and something just . . . pops. Like their brain short-circuits, and they do this mad act and wonder how they ever did it once it's all over." That wasn't strictly true. Tracy knew damn well why she'd killed — and she didn't feel an ounce of remorse over it. No, John had been a filthy, depraved bastard, and he didn't deserve *any* justice. She didn't have to wonder why she'd done it at all.

If only there was a law that allowed people to get away with killing their abusers.

"Still doesn't justify it, though," Gilbert said.

Would he say the same if Tracy told him her story? The *real* story?

"I suppose not, but I do have sympathy for some killers. Those who have it in their nature, no, but those who have been nurtured in a terrible life and become someone who kills? Yes." Those words came out sharper than she would have liked.

Gilbert stared at her, his eyebrows raised. "That sounded a bit passionate."

"I see the other side of the fence," she said. He could take from that what he fancied. "It's not always black and white. There are colours, so many of them, and so deep, most people wouldn't understand unless they've been there."

"Have you?" He rested a hand on her upper arm.

"I'll tell you a bit about myself one day. Then you'll understand what I mean."

"Oh . . ."

"Indeed." She clapped once, the gloves muffling the slap of skin on skin. "Right. Time to be getting on."

"An adept way to avoid a conversation if ever I heard one." He grinned, but it didn't reach his soulful eyes.

Tracy had to turn away from them.

"You've been terribly hurt, haven't you?" he asked, squeezing her arm gently.

"You could say that." She stared at the body instead of him. "But I'm getting help. Finally. Tonight, after work. Someone to talk to. It's time to let it all go."

"Good." He took his hand away. "Ah, before you toddle off. ID. She had some on her."

Shit, I forgot to ask. "Good."

"Although it doesn't show her age . . ." He bent over to take a clear evidence bag containing a bank card out of a box a foot or so from the body. "A Miss J Locke."

Could it still be Lisa with a new name?

She was wicked — hideous and wicked — for hoping it was.

"Won't be hard to find her from that," she said. "Nationwide Building Society might help us out if we can't find her ourselves. Damon . . ." She twisted to see where he was. In the corner talking to a SOCO. "Can you get hold of Nada about this, please?"

Gilbert waved the evidence bag then strode over there, probably so Damon wouldn't have to come near the body.

Tracy studied the victim a bit more to get her head on straight. She'd thought some nasty things in the space of about ten minutes and had to process how she felt about them. She always justified her actions and thoughts by blaming the Past — she'd said as much to Gilbert — but surely there had to come a time when she must blame herself. Not everything she said and did stemmed from *there*, did it? Could her attitude today — all of it — be attributed to what she'd been through?

That was a question for the shrink. One she may or may not ask. It would depend on her state of mind once she'd met the woman.

"Um, boss?" Damon.

"Yes?" She jumped and whipped her head around to look at him, the action telling her she felt guilty for her thoughts. Otherwise, why would she have started like that? "What's up?" She was back in detective mode, leaving the unsure and mean Tracy behind — until the next time she was faced with something she didn't like and acidic crap came spewing out of her mouth.

"Nada needs to have a word." Damon held the phone out.

Tracy passed Gilbert returning to the body, and she took the phone. "Hi, Nada."

"Got a hit on some fingerprints in Mrs Roberts' bedroom at Blooming Age, boss."

"Brilliant. Who do they belong to?"

"An unknown person."

"Eh? How's that?"

"Well, there are prints in the database for crimes where no one knows who those prints belong to."

Tracy could have kicked herself. Of course there were unknown prints on file. She *knew* that. "Sorry. Lost the plot for a second there." *Because my mind is elsewhere.* "What case do they relate to?"

"That's just it, boss. Um . . . I did a search, and I see you're the only Tracy Collier so . . ."

Oh fuck. No. Hell no. Not this . . . please don't tell me it's . . .

"As far as I'm aware, I am . . ." Would her legs even hold her up through this call? They shook, and it seemed her blood had frozen. Sweat prickled on the back of her neck.

"Just that they were found in a house that belonged to a Collier, and I looked him up, and your name . . . Well, you're his daughter?"

Tracy swallowed. Willed herself not to go down on her knees in fear. "I know what case that is. Surprised you didn't know about it already. It was all over the news. I was the lead on it." *I was the reason for it, for the murders.*

"Yes, I know the case," Nada said. "I just didn't twig you were his daughter."

"So, the fingerprints . . . They can't be my father's or mother's — they're dead — and my sister ran away after I was born, hasn't been seen since."

All those lies, back again.

Nada cleared her throat. "It says on file that these fingerprints belong to a woman suspected of living with . . . uh . . . your father at that time." She sounded incredibly uncomfortable.

"Look, let's acknowledge the white elephant, all right? My father killed people. If you've read the file, followed the case, you'll know I left home as soon as I could and didn't have anything to do with him from that day onwards. What he did is nothing to do with me." *It has everything to do with me.* "I'd appreciate it, though, if you don't allow the team to gossip about this when they also find out these details. Let me tell them this particular story."

"Whatever you want, boss. I'm . . . shit, I'm so sorry."

"No need to be. He was a bastard. I'm over it." *No, I'm not.* "We treat this new finding like any other. A lead. So, the woman suspected of living with my father — who, by the way, ran off after she killed my old chief — has now resurfaced in this town." *Had to get that nugget in about Lisa killing John.* "Good. Means we can question her when we find her and ask her about the Collier case, too — and the Spinks debacle." *Please, God, say we won't find her.*

"Okay. What do you need me to do about this . . . information?"

"Get on to the lab and chivvy them along to see if the hair on the pillow matches any hairs found at the Collier house. Tell them it's high priority, that we need to know so we can stop a killer."

"Okay. Are you . . . are you really all right, though, boss? I mean, this is a hell of a case, the one with your father, and I'm worried—"

"I appreciate your concern, Nada, I do, but let's not even go there. It's . . ."

"Too much?"

"Yes. Maybe one day . . . maybe one day I'll tell you a few things. When we're closer. That might take years for us to get to that point, as I don't trust easily, so don't hold your breath." *Why am I opening up all of a sudden?* Twice she'd offered to tell colleagues her story now — a story she told herself she'd keep hidden. Maybe going to the therapist was why. She knew she'd have to open up to her, too. Shrugging, as though that would knock the ever-present chips off her shoulders as well as the weight of her actual lies, she said, "Gilbert thinks the same knife was used on this victim — the same as on Irene Roberts."

"Bloody hell . . ."

"I know. So get the team on finding out who this lady is — Locke — and look into her life. The usual shit — friends, family, Facebook, bank accounts." Tracy wanted to end the call, to be left alone for a moment. She wasn't in the mood to do anything now except wonder: *Why the fuck was Lisa in Irene Roberts' room?*

And: *Should I tell Damon now or later?*

"We'll be back in a bit," she told Nada, cutting the call and glancing at Damon to find him staring at her, his mouth slightly open, his brow scrunched. He'd been listening to her side of the convo, then.

Shit.

"We need to get back," she said to him. "I gather from your expression you heard?"

"I did. So she's back on the scene, that bitch who stabbed me."

"Seems so." Tracy wanted to sigh all her troubles away. They were here to stay, though — for now. She had to get a break at some point, didn't she? Life was an overexcited monkey slinging crap through the bars that caged her in. Could it keep throwing it? How long before she crumbled?

"We'd better fucking catch her this time," Damon said, voice hard, his face hardening, too.

We'd better fucking not . . . "Here's hoping," she said. "Come on. We've got to get back so I can explain this mess to the team. I didn't think I'd have to talk to them about what we've been through, but . . ."

She waved goodbye to Gilbert and left the tent, sucking in air, which was thick with humidity and swirled heavily in her lungs. A cold drink was in order, so she jerked her head in the direction of the alley, and Damon walked down it beside her.

"We need to go and nose out here, at the road opposite," she said. "That's where the sex workers tout from. Bit of luck, there might be one out there now. Daylight doesn't bother them these days."

At the mouth of the alley, she paused. "We'll go to Costa and watch from there."

They walked to the shop, and inside, Tracy picked up a bottle of water for a price that could have bought a six-pack in Asda. Damon had a coffee. They sat at a table by the window so she could stare out — anything to avoid looking into Damon's eyes at the moment.

"Are you all right?" he asked.

She should have been asking *him* that question. After all, it was him her sister had stabbed. "So-so. You?"

"Angry. Excited that we might finally collar her. Hacked off that she might have killed Mrs Roberts — and, going by listening to Gilbert back at the scene, that poor woman in the car park. What the fuck is wrong with her? We never did work out a proper reason why she stabbed me, did we."

"No — except for the fact it was to get at me for some reason." She unscrewed the lid of her water and guzzled a few swallows, hating herself for once again bullshitting Damon. "My father probably told her a load of crap about me, and that's why she went after you. Who knows why these people do stuff like that." *I can't even ask him to leave it, to stop talking about it this time. She's in our lives again — both of ours — to do with work.*

"When we catch her, I'm going to ask her so many questions," he said.

We won't catch her, not if I have anything to do with it.

"And why is she even here, in this town?" he went on. "It was *definitely* her we saw that time. I wish I'd bloody caught her when I chased her."

I don't. I'm glad you didn't.

"And as for her changing her MO," he said. "What's that all about? I mean, she gutted her last victim — the last we know about anyway — same as she tried to do with me, so why move to slitting throats?"

"I don't know."

Had Lisa got herself into some sort of network, like Tracy had suggested to Gilbert? Had she been sent to kill Irene Roberts? And the Locke woman — was she another sex worker, and if so, had Lisa had fallen out with her?

Tracy would find out sooner or later, but she didn't want to.

Fuck, no.

CHAPTER SIXTEEN

There's that knocking again. It's annoying, because I don't know where it's coming from. Next door on the right are usually a quiet couple, rarely a peep out of them most of the time, and the left — well, he's not there that often, although he is at the moment. He works away somewhere abroad for stretches at a time, then comes back for a week or two. Our houses aren't joined anyway, so I can't blame him.

It's not the same here now. I think I'm the only resident left in the street from when I was a kid. There's no one to have a chat with about the old days. They're either dead or have moved away to better houses, better lives.

I don't feel right since the Mrs Roberts business. Out of sorts, but I suppose I could put it down to the events that took place. I wish we hadn't fallen asleep. Then we would have checked the rooms regularly, every half an hour like we're meant to. And Zello is blaming me, I know she is. That dig about it being down to me because I was in charge that night . . . it hurt, but it was the truth.

It is my fault.

It was a stupid idea to give the nurses a bit of down-time. I shouldn't have suggested it. The only reason I did was because of how Mrs Roberts had been behaving. No one enjoys going into work when there's someone who makes those hours difficult.

I'm not sure why she went all funny either. She's usually a decent sort, if a bit anxious, looking around her all the time at everyone, as though she's trying to spot a face she recognises, maybe someone from her family. Then she started wanting to go outside, to get away from her room, from the building, because she said a man had come in and threatened her. *And* she stopped coming to the dining room to have her meals with everyone else. It seemed a sudden change in her, and I can't work it out.

The other day, she'd said to me, "I don't like him." I didn't know who she meant, so asked if it was Nurse Matthews she was on about, but she'd said, "No, not him. *Him.*" So I'd asked about the man in the van, Martin, and she said he was nice, although he reminded her of a fella she used to know years ago. She didn't say anything more about that when I pressed her.

So a man had upset her, and that only leaves the two gardeners or the owner of the care home, and he doesn't visit except once in the spring and then near Christmas, so it can't be him.

When I'm next at work, I'm going to ask about the gardeners, see if anyone knows anything. I have no idea who they are, seeing as I work nights.

I can't help but think I ought to know the man Mrs Roberts was on about.

That knocking is back.

I close my eyes to hear it better, to judge where it's coming from. It's faint, far away but not, and it seems to be coming from below. In the basement? I haven't been down there for years. Maybe there's a rat or something, brushing against stuff.

Yes. It's a rat. That's what it is.

CHAPTER SEVENTEEN

"Do we have anything new?" Tracy asked, walking into the incident room, out of breath at those three flights of bloody stairs. They killed her calf muscles something chronic. She stood in front of the whiteboards and examined the job sheets. A second set had been tacked beside the first and contained information on the Locke woman. "Ah, I see we have progress with finding out who she was. Locke, I mean. Jasmine. Nice name." She turned to face her crew.

Nada got out of her chair to sit on the edge of her desk. "Yes, Jasmine Locke, twenty-nine, sex worker by night, mother by day."

"Shit." Tracy scrunched her eyes shut. So Jasmine was one of the few who didn't bear the stomach scars from being pregnant. "How many kids?" She sighed.

"Three."

Eyes open, she widened them at Nada. "Father around?"

"Yes. Well, he's got the same address as her anyway."

"He didn't report her missing?"

"Checked that, boss. No."

"Either he was used to her not coming home, or he didn't want to phone in because of her profession. Might not have wanted to get her in the shit." Tracy pinched her bottom lip.

"And probably because she's on the social," Tim said. "It came up in the search. Only applied for it two weeks ago. If she's earning extra money and not declaring it, which she can't really if she's selling sex, if he rang up and told us what she was actually doing last night . . ."

"Yes, that might have stopped him calling it in. What a shame." Tracy held back another sigh. "If he had, we might have stood more chance of catching her killer. Any luck with CCTV in the warehouse area and roads leading up to it?"

"None outside the warehouses," Lara said around the end of a pen in her mouth. "That whole area there is abandoned. CCTV cuts off a few streets away. All I've seen so far on the roads before the cutoff are cars. I've been able to find the owners of — two women, three men — a cyclist, looked like a bloke, seventeen pedestrians, and four taxis. I still need to deal with the latter set."

"Right, thanks, although good luck on finding the cyclist and pedestrians. No chance unless we put out an appeal. Anything else?" Tracy asked.

"She didn't enter via the alley — she's not on CCTV there," Alastair said. "She wasn't even on that sex-worker patch. Maybe she was on the other one."

"That's good," Tracy said. "We can concentrate our efforts on the one in Jester Street then. Bloody good work, guys." She felt as though they were getting somewhere — with Locke's case anyway. "I have a little something to tell you before we move on." She took a deep breath. "Nada discovered that fingerprints from Mrs Roberts' room match those in another case, although the owner of those prints is an unknown." She ploughed on, telling them the official story of the Collier case and leaving out the huge chunks of truth. Obviously. "So, you can see why this one is a little bit important to us. Not just for me, because of it being related to me in the ways I explained, but because that cow stabbed Damon. She needs catching, as soon as." *She doesn't. She really doesn't . . .* "Let's get cracking on this and see what turns up next. Damon, you and me — we're off to see the father of

Locke's kids and find out if they were together or he's just dossing there."

"Might be her pimp," Erica said. "Maybe that's why he didn't call her in as missing."

"That's not a bad assumption," Tracy said. "I'll bear that in mind when I question him. Any specs on him?" She knew there would be. Her team were shit-hot — she was proud to have them on her side.

"Yes," Erica said, turning to her monitor. She clicked a few buttons. "Pete Hewson, thirty-one, lives at sixty-five Minton Gardens. Priors are being in possession of weed — not enough to get him banged up — a drunk and disorderly, an aggravated assault; charges were dropped on that one. Basically, he's possibly a bit of trouble but not a major pest. He hasn't done anything wrong since he was twenty, so eleven years as a good boy."

"Right." Tracy walked up to Erica's desk to have a nose at Hewson's picture. Caucasian, blond, and he liked the gym according to the size of his neck; several cords and veins stood out. Steroid user? She'd bet his body was beefy, wide, and heavy. "Okay . . . Nice tattoo peeking out of his T-shirt there. Looks like the top of a Celtic cross. Anyway, we must get going." On her way to the door, she said over her shoulder, "On you go. Let's get this sorted sooner rather than later in case the killer decides to do it again." *And if it's Lisa, she will.*

I don't know what to do. I'm actually at a loss. Before, it seemed clear-cut — keep Lisa out of sight and eventually it would all go away. But now? Shit.

She left the room, stopped to chat for a moment with Vic on the front desk while waiting for Damon to catch up, then headed to her car. She scanned the area for any sign of Lisa lurking around, hoping her perusal appeared natural. Damon didn't comment, so she guessed she'd been successful.

She was a master at covering up.

The drive to Minton Gardens didn't take long, and Tracy didn't speak on the way. She didn't want to slip up and say something wrong — not until she'd had a chance to filter through today's information then lock things away in her head properly. And he seemed pensive anyway, probably thinking of all the things he'd say to Lisa when he sat in front of her in an interview.

Of course, Winter could insist Tracy and Damon were too close, too involved, and he might take over, sitting in with Nada to question Lisa, leaving Damon and Tracy to watch in another room, Tracy crapping herself every time Lisa opened her spiteful little mouth.

Just thinking about that scenario and the truths Lisa would spill to get Tracy in trouble had her shivering. But Damon . . . he deserved closure, for Lisa to be caught.

So why couldn't Tracy allow it to happen? Why wasn't that a good reason for her to arrest Lisa herself when she next saw her? Didn't she love Damon enough, was that it? Did she love herself more? Or was it self-preservation taking over, not allowing her to do anything even if she wanted to?

Tracy was a nasty piece of work, that was all there was to it.

That therapist had better help me, because, shit, I can't even help the man I'm supposed to care about. I'd say I can't even help myself, but I seem to be doing a pretty good job of it so far.

I hate that part of me, the one Damon has no clue exists.

She turned into Minton Gardens, a quiet cul-de-sac with detached houses, nice lawns out the front. How did Jasmine afford to live here?

Stupid question if she was raking in the cash at night . . .

The homes looked to be four or five beds, spacious, and would cost a packet to buy and run. Pale-brown bricks with black, mock-Tudor beams on the top half. Large windows with diamond lead. Perhaps they private rented, and the rent was paid through housing benefit. That had to be the case if Jasmine was on the social. Even the council tax would be close to two hundred a month.

Outside number sixty-five, Tracy parked and copped a peek at Damon while he stared left at the houses on the other side of the street. What was he thinking? Did she even want to know?

Not really.

"You okay?" she asked, more because she sort of had to than anything else.

He turned to look at her. "We're so close to getting hold of her. It feels like it'll come to an end now, then I think about how she keeps getting away and I worry she'll do it again. It's actually making me ill, Trace."

Oh God . . .

"What do you mean, ill?" Her stomach flipped over.

"Nerves. I might have to go and see someone. I get jittery sometimes. Like I've had too much coffee, except I haven't. I'm not right. Not the same as I was. I think about her sometimes. At night. When you're asleep. And it's like she's there, in the room with us."

If that didn't make her feel guilty, she didn't know what would. And if it didn't make her want to find Lisa and take her down to the station, she was a bitch of the highest order. Hell, she knew she was. She'd already shoved aside the fact he'd been stabbed by her sister. That should have been enough for Tracy to want to arrest her.

Obviously, it wasn't. Did Damon have to be dead for her to do that?

Sodding hell . . .

"See someone?" she parroted.

"A doctor. I'm not doing as well as I led you to believe. I hate keeping things from you. It isn't right. Sorry for lying."

Damon, you have no idea how your one lie is drowned by my million.

"It's okay," she said, reaching out to put her hand on his thigh. "We all have things we keep to ourselves. We're going to catch her. We are." *I am. And I'm going to fucking kill her.* "Let's get this interview out of the way, then we can think about how we're going to catch her, all right?" *Why didn't I write Lisa's number down before I deleted her messages? I could have arranged to meet her.*

"Yep. Once she's caught, I'll be fine. It's just . . . I keep thinking about it. The stabbing. Her face. Her eyes . . ."

"Jesus. Do you need to see a therapist again? Someone other than one appointed by work? What about making an appointment to have a chat with mine? Or you could wait until I've been later, so I can tell you what she's like?"

He nodded. "I think I might have to, love."

She rested her temple on his shoulder and hugged his arm. "I'm so very sorry about all this." *But I wasn't sorry enough until now. Always thinking of myself.* "If I could turn the clock back . . ."

"But you can't. It's done. We just have to nab her before she does it again, because it's looking like she did Irene Roberts and Jasmine Locke. I'd hate to think what's going through her head and—" He sat straighter. "Fucking hell!"

"What?" Tracy bolted up beside him, looking in all directions out of the windows. "I don't see anything."

"No, I just had a thought. There was me saying she'd changed her MO, but she didn't. She hasn't *changed* it this time, just used one of two."

"What do you mean?" Tracy's heartrate went mental. What was he getting at? What had she missed — or forgotten?

"She guts people but also slits their throats."

"That's obvious, what with Irene and Jasmine . . ."

"John," he said.

And that one word floated on Damon's breath, crept down Tracy's throat, and strangled her. She needed to get out of the car. To run. To be anywhere but here. The urge to escape was massive, but she fought it and won. Controlling her breathing, she said, "My God . . ."

"Exactly. I'm telling you, it's her doing this, Trace. Even without the evidence of her fingerprints in Roberts' room, I know it's her. And you can bet they're her clothes, too, the ones found in the back garden at Blooming Age, though why they have shit on the jeans is anyone's guess."

He was right. They would be Lisa's. Cruella de Fate wouldn't allow them to belong to anyone else. But how had Lisa been strong enough to carry an old lady? All right, she'd had immense strength in the past when she'd killed all those people before, so maybe that wasn't such a far-fetched idea that she'd be able to haul Mrs Roberts out to a car. But why kill her? What the hell had Mrs Roberts ever done to her?

What did all her other victims ever do? Nothing. Wrong place, wrong time.

And why had she left her clothes there? Was it like the scarf she'd folded and placed on her victim before? Had she wanted Tracy to know it was her? A reminder of the rainbow scarf in their childhood? To goad her, to see if Tracy would finally, *finally* buckle and haul Lisa in? Maybe Lisa was testing Tracy, seeing if she loved her. Tracy could relate to that behaviour. She was bad to Damon a lot of the time, so was she testing him, too. Waiting to see how far she could go before he stopped caring?

She was more like her sister than she cared to admit.

"What a fucking mess," she said, and she didn't mean the case as a whole either.

"And then some. Come on. We have a job to do."

He got out of the car, leaving her staring after him as he shut the door then walked to the pavement.

"I've got to find her and get rid of her," she said, glad Damon couldn't see her lips moving, what with his back facing her. That was all she needed, him thinking she wasn't right in the head.

But she wasn't, was she, and that was the damn problem.

CHAPTER EIGHTEEN

On the step in front of a mahogany door with a black handle, letterbox, lion's head knocker, and no window, Tracy pressed the brass bell button on the frame to the right. Damon stood just behind her, and she glanced over her shoulder at him. He smiled, and she took that to mean he was all right now. He was going to be okay.

She was unbelievably happy about that. If the idea of catching Lisa brightened his spirits, what would he be like if they actually nabbed her?

She ought to want to do that, so he would be at peace.

The door opened, and straight away, Tracy launched into her spiel. "Mr Hewson? DI Tracy Collier and DS Damon Hanks. We're here about Jasmine Locke. Can we come in?"

Hewson didn't resemble his mugshot. He looked more like a young Hulk Hogan now. Oiled or gelled, swept-back long hair and a thick, banana-coloured moustache. Grey T-shirt over a broad chest with hard pecs. Black jeans, his thighs wider than Tracy's two put together. His eyes narrowed quickly, as though he debated his options.

Truth or lie?

Tracy waited to see which one would come out of his mouth.

"Bloody hell." He said it on a gust of breath. "Get herself caught, did she?" He sighed as though he'd expected them to pop round. "Come in." He moved aside, bare feet *shushing* on the beech laminate flooring.

They entered, and he shut the door, the hallway going dark. A slice of light came from an archway on the left — sunlight, not artificial.

"I told her to pack it in," he said, folding his arms across the top of his flat belly, "but she wouldn't listen. It's one of the reasons we split up. I had a feeling she'd been picked up by you lot when she didn't make it home. I come and see the kids some evenings, see, look after them while she goes out, otherwise I wouldn't be here this time of day. I normally leave once she gets back about three in the morning. We parted ways about two weeks ago — split up, like."

Tracy didn't fancy having this conversation in the gloomy hallway, albeit it one the size of a small bedroom with a tasteful sideboard, flowers in a clear, rectangular vase on top.

Who bought them? A new fella?

"Like flowers, do you?" Hewson asked. "Jas does. I buy them every week. Thought I'd carry on even though we're not together. They make her happy. I'd do anything to make her happy."

Oh no . . .

Tracy had the ridiculous urge to cry. "Can we go and sit down?"

"Oh, yes. Sorry. Want a cuppa, do you? I was just about to have a coffee myself."

"That would be nice. Thank you."

They followed him into the kitchen, a modern one with all the bells and whistles — lots of black and chrome, a built-in dishwasher humming and swishing. He got three sun-yellow cups out of a cupboard and lifted a full coffee carafe from the shiny black machine beside a silver kettle.

"I'm meant to be at work," he said. "I had to call in sick. Someone had to get the kids to school and clean this place up. She's let it slide since I moved out. Was a bit of a pigsty last night, to be honest. Don't think the landlord would be too pleased, know what I mean?" He looked over at them. "Shit, got no manners. Sit down if you want."

Tracy took a seat on one side of a black ash table. Damon remained standing by the open back door; the rear garden was mainly grass, no flowerbeds, and a shed right at the bottom. A pink bike rested on its side in the middle of the lawn. The sunlight had been coming from this room into the hallway, then, through that arch.

The day was another scorcher. Washing hung on a rotary line, unmoving, baking away in the heat. Children's clothes mainly, and a quilt cover with the characters from *Paw Patrol* on it. Hewson must be a domestic sort, unless Jasmine had pegged it out yesterday and hadn't got it in before she'd left the house.

"What time did Jasmine go out last night?" she finally asked.

Hewson carried two cups to the table and placed them on brushed steel coasters. Damon lifted a hand when Hewson turned to get the other one on the countertop and collected it himself.

"Thanks," Hewson said and plonked himself on a chair opposite Tracy.

He was so big, she wondered how the chair didn't creak. Hewson was all muscle, his biceps bulging beneath his T-shirt sleeves, half of a tattoo hiding beneath the material. She checked his neckline. The top of what she'd assumed was a Celtic cross on his arrest picture looked more like part of an intricate circle now. Maybe he'd added to it since that photo had been taken.

"Um, she left about eight," Hewson said. "I know that because the kids have to be asleep by then. Routine — helps them in the long run. I got here about seven so I could give them a bath and tuck them in while she got ready. Why? You can ask her yourself, surely."

Tracy smiled tightly. "And she was going where?"

"Out on the lash, so she told me, but I'm thinking she didn't. Not if you're here. What, is she getting banged up for a spell now, so you need to see if anyone can have the kids? No need. I'll do it. Maybe this will teach her a lesson. Not being funny, like, but I did tell her she'd get caught one day."

"Caught doing what, Mr Hewson?"

He frowned. "Don't you know? Soliciting, you call it. I'd called it spreading her legs for money when she had a perfectly good bloke at home who was willing and earned enough to keep us. I mean, look at this place. I afforded it all on my wages — electrician. I said she'd come a cropper one day, and once I left and she had to go on the dole, I told her she'd get caught fiddling the social if she carried on doing what she did. I'm only telling you what you must already know, otherwise, why are you here? I wouldn't normally say anything negative about her — I still love her — but she's got to learn you can't do what she does and get away with it, can you?"

"No," Tracy said. "However, her being on the social and earning extra money by selling sex isn't why we're here. Do you have anyone other than the children who can verify you were here all night?"

He nodded. "Bit of a weird question, isn't it? What does it matter what I was doing? As it happens, my mates came round. We had a few games on the PlayStation, a couple of beers. One of them stayed over on the sofa, left about ten minutes before you arrived, actually. And next door will tell you they were here, because he was meant to come and all, but he nipped round about half eight to say his missus had a shit fit about it, so he didn't bother. He lives at sixty-four. Tom Berns. You can go and ask him now if you like. He's got a week off work. He's out doing a bit of gardening. I said I'd help him later."

"We'll go and see him after we leave here." She picked up her coffee, blew it, and took a sip. Cup back on the table, she asked, "Does Jasmine work for herself or for someone else, if you see what I mean?"

"As far as I know, she just went out and waited with all the other women. I put up with it for ages, and lately, she didn't go out so much, so I assumed she'd stopped. Then she went out again, and I knew what she'd been up to because she had a shower when she got back. I lost it a bit, and we had a row. That's when I left. If she had a pimp or whatever they're called these days, I'd have known about it." He frowned. "I think. Although I didn't know what she was up to in that regard for a good year or two, so scrap that." He ran a finger along his moustache. "Look, what's happening? If I need to move in here for a bit while she does a few weeks in the nick, that's fine. You don't need to be telling the social services or anything. They're my kids, and I'll look after them. My mum will help."

"Why is your name still listed as you living here?" Tracy asked. Stalling. Not wanting to deliver the News. She liked Hewson and didn't want to watch him break down.

"Haven't got around to changing it. Like I said, I only left about a fortnight ago. I'm at Mum's for now. I kind of hoped Jas would change her evening behaviour, for want of a better way of putting it, and we'd get back together. Seemed stupid to switch everything over if I was only going to be coming back." He shook his head. "She's a daft mare, but I bloody love her, you know?"

It was so obvious he did. And for him to want her back despite the 'career' choice she'd made — well, it spoke volumes. Tracy ought to just tell him now. Get it over and done with. Break his heart.

Poor bastard.

"Mr Hewson, I regret to have to inform you that—"

"No. Oh fucking no. You're not here for that." He scraped his chair back and paced, shoving a hand through his hair and disrupting the gelled comb lines. "No. Not Jas . . ."

"I'm afraid so," Tracy said.

"What am I going to tell the kids? They're only nippers. Fuck me . . ." He flopped down into his seat again, whimpering, elbows on the table, forehead resting in his hands. His breaths came out ragged.

Tracy opted to remain silent while the man processed the news. She peered over her shoulder at Damon, who looked distraught. He hated this part of the job.

She returned her attention to Hewson.

When he lifted his head, tears tracked down his cheeks and disappeared into his moustache. "How?" That one word was broken, rasped out, and he stared at her with watery, pleading eyes.

This is so fucking awful.

"She was murdered."

He swallowed, gawping at her, clearly unable to comprehend what she'd said. The stare-off lasted about a minute, then, "You what? By a punter? Are you saying some bloke went with her, then he . . ."

"We don't know yet, sorry to say. She was found this morning."

"What did he do to her?"

Don't be too sure it's a he . . .

"She'd had her throat cut." Tracy winced at his face crumpling.

"Bloody hell . . . Oh God . . . Who the fuck would want to do something like that to my Jas?" He lowered his hands to the table. His fingers shook, tapping away, his pinkie rattling one of the coasters. "I mean, I know some people get killed while doing what she does, and that's what bothered me the most about her doing it — not that she was cheating on me — but *Jasmine*?"

"That's what we aim to find out — who did it and why," Tracy said.

More tears came then, and he let them fall, closing his eyes.

Tracy sipped her coffee and waited, managing to drink half a cup.

Then he looked at her again.

His expression tugged at her heart.

Don't lose it now. Not after all these years of being a hard cow.

"We'll find whoever did it. I can't promise it will be now — sometimes it takes weeks, months — but we'll get them eventually." She hadn't said *years* — that would be too much of a kick in the teeth.

"That's no good to me or the kids, is it, *getting* them? He's done the worst he can do to us, so what does it matter now?"

"It matters in case this person does it to someone else, which means other partners, children, mums and dads, sisters and brothers, will be without the person they love."

Shame you didn't think about that before now, Collier. You let her go, and look what she's done. What you've done.

"Oh . . ." He shook his head.

"This person may also have killed someone else recently before Jasmine, so it really is important we find them before they do it again. Do you know of anyone who would have wanted to do this to her?"

"What do you mean?" He frowned, as though what she'd said was difficult to understand.

"Is there anyone who might hold a grudge, maybe disliked her, things along those lines?"

"Jasmine? No! She was lovely. I've known her since school. We started going out when we were thirteen. She wouldn't hurt anyone. I might not have liked it that she went on the game, but I tried to help her get off it, I really did."

"I don't doubt you, Mr Hewson. I'm going to have to leave you now and visit Jasmine's mother." *I've done it again. Not looked up the next of kin. Told the wrong person first.*

"No need. She's dead."

Thank God.

"When was that?"

"A few months before Jas started going out at night to do . . . that."

"Might explain her behaviour," Tracy said. "Some people deal with grief in unusual ways."

"That's why I put up with it at first, but when it extended to years . . ."

"Does she have a father?"

"No. She never knew him."

"Siblings?"

"No. An aunt. She lives in Croydon. Jessica Usherton. No idea where she lives in Croydon, though. We don't speak to her much. Jas's family all have J names. Her mum was Janine." The last word went up a scale or two, and it was clear he was fighting to keep it together.

She didn't have to ask why he'd told her that, about the names. People in his position sometimes said the most inane things, possibly the way the mind helped the grieving to cope, splashing random things out there to save them thinking of other, more horrifying subjects.

"Why don't you bring up your mum's number on your phone, and DS Hanks will give her a ring for you." She held her hand out. People tended to do as she asked if she made it clear she wouldn't take anything less than their obedience.

He did as told, keying in his password then passing the phone over. Tracy gave it to Damon and inclined her head towards the hallway. Damon left the room and closed the door behind him.

"Mr Hewson, if Jasmine's aunt doesn't want to identify her body, would you—"

"No. No, I can't see her like . . . like that. Not if she's had her throat cut. I can't . . ."

She reached out and took hold of his hand. "I understand. I'm sure Ms Usherton will do it." She thought of Jasmine's swollen, bruised face and wondered how anyone would be able to identify her anyway.

He stared at her as though his mind had gone blank, so she sat with him in silence until Damon came back. Then she took her hand away.

"Your mother will be here in a minute, Mr Hewson," Damon said. "She was on her way already. Apparently had some sixth sense and knew something was wrong."

Tracy glanced at Damon — could Hewson's mother have done it? He shook his head.

How did he always know what she was thinking?

Not always. If he did, he'd have left your arse long ago.

Fuck off.

"Did your mother know about what Jasmine did?" Tracy asked.

"God, no. She'd have a fit." Hewson rubbed his cheeks and said behind his palms, "And I'm not telling her either. Unless it makes the news. Shit." He dropped his hands to his lap.

"It's bound to," Tracy said, "although we'll try to keep it quiet for as long as possible. We may have to turn to the press for help at some point, though."

"The kids. They're going to find out. They'll get picked on at school." He looked like a kid himself. Lost. Vulnerable. Suddenly smaller than he was.

"That's possible, I'm afraid. People aren't too kind regarding certain things. It's going to be a tough road ahead," she said.

"I'll move. Take them somewhere new. They don't need this on top of losing their mother."

Satisfied that Hewson wasn't anyone they needed to keep an eye on, Tracy rose, and the doorbell rang. Damon went to answer and returned with a woman in her sixties, short blonde hair like Mo from *Eastenders*, the same sort of face, too.

"What's going on?" she asked.

So Damon hadn't told her on the phone then.

Tracy waited for two heartbeats to see if she or Damon needed to answer her.

They didn't.

"It's Jas, Mum. She's dead."

Mrs Hewson fainted.

CHAPTER NINETEEN

The rest of the day was spent in the incident room, everyone working quietly to pull all the information together. The team rubbed along well, and Tracy couldn't be happier with how they'd gelled. If she were honest, they were tighter than her previous crew, and she never thought she'd be able to say that when she'd first taken over this squad. With their old boss, Kane, out of the picture, and the first few hiccups dealt with swiftly, things had evened out.

They could only grow stronger as time went by.

Four o'clock approached, and Tracy stood from her seat beside Damon at his desk and nipped to her office to type out her notes for today. Twenty-five minutes later, to refresh her mind, she returned to the incident room and read through the information on the whiteboards that had been added in the last few hours.

"Right, down tools," she said. "It's almost time to go — well, half an hour yet — and as we haven't got anything to go on with regards to finding our suspect, name unknown, we won't be putting in any overtime — except for you, Nada and Erica. I want you to go out and speak to the sex workers tonight, if you haven't got anything else on this evening."

"Fine by me," Nada said.

"Same here," Erica replied. "Just a pile of ironing waiting for me at home, so working is preferable, thanks."

Titters from everyone, then silence.

"It only needs a couple of hours," Tracy said. "Say between eight and ten, the spot in Jester Street." She pointed to the task sheets for Jasmine Locke. "It seems this is the part of the case we're better off following to find leads. Mrs Roberts' trail has gone cold . . . ish. Apart from knowing our suspect was in her room, and getting word from forensics that it's looking likely the hair on the pillow is also from the same person the fingerprints belong to, we've got sod all else on that front. Jasmine Locke, however . . . We have the sex workers to talk to, and we know she was there in Jester Street because we've spotted her on CCTV, thank fuck. She got into a taxi, right, so now we need to find that taxi. As Tim found out earlier, all but one of the four taxis spotted on the CCTV in the warehouse vicinity have been ruled out. They were on jobs, proof supplied. The other taxi, though . . . It has to be the one Jasmine got in, agreed?"

Murmurs of dissent went around.

"Okay, you're probably right, it might not be, but I'm trying to give us some hope here. So, tomorrow, we look into where this taxi could have been purchased. Or did someone buy the light that goes on top and have stickers printed off for the doors?" *Lisa wouldn't go to all that trouble, would she? Plus, she's skint — or she was last time we got chatting about money.* "Remember, the word 'taxi' was on the doors in white. We need to see if letters were bought in somewhere like Rymans or WHSmith — you know, like you can buy sticky-backed numbers for wheelie bins."

"I'll do that tonight," Damon said. What he didn't say was he'd do it while waiting for her to come back from seeing the therapist. "I'd rather try to find this fucker now. If we leave it until tomorrow, he — or *she* — could kill again in the meantime."

"Okay, I've got somewhere to be, but I'll come back and join you afterwards." Tracy wasn't about to let the team know where she was off to. "If we can get something from that taxi search, we might well get a lead on the driver, which means an arrest is imminent. If me and Damon can handle that, though, I won't bother you lot, so don't go home and sit there on edge, waiting for me to call."

More murmurs, excited this time.

"We'll get whoever it is, guys, we just have a lot of grunt work to do beforehand, unfortunately. So, get yourselves off now — yes, it's early, I know — and get a good night's sleep. Nada, Erica, thank you for putting in the extra hours without giving me grief over it."

Everyone packed their things away and shut down computers. Tracy nipped to Winter's office to let him know the latest, then she went back to the incident room, which was now empty except for Damon. He was searching up what Rymans sold and writing things down on a pad.

"I need to go," she said, coming up behind him, bending and giving him a hug, their cheeks pressed together.

He rested his head on her arm then and held her hand, his palm warm and comforting. "You'll be fine, won't you?"

"I have to be. I can't keep going like this." Truth be told — *blimey, I'm not lying for once?* — she was bricking it.

"It's not going away, is it?" he said. "Like for me."

"No, it's here to stay if I don't get it sorted." *And maybe I won't need to go there after tonight if I find Lisa, stop her doing anything else for good. Shit, and it's not all about me. Damon can't keep living like this either.* She took a deep breath. "Okay, I'm going now. Don't see me out. I'm fine. You keep doing what you're doing."

She left him there and dashed down the stairs — not because she couldn't wait to get there, but because if she didn't rush, she'd bottle it and not go at all. She waved to Vic on the front desk then got into her car, belting out onto the road and merging into the traffic. The normality of it, creeping along behind people going home after a long day, eased her nerves a little. She couldn't help but think about Dr Fuckface — George Schumer — her old therapist. He'd been . . . killed.

He could have fixed me. I could have been a proper person by now instead of this evil mess.

She pulled up outside the therapist's practise, nothing like Fuckface's, which had been a house in a former life. This one was a huge glass-fronted building, that glass tinted blue, the ghostly silhouettes of people going about their business inside. Three stories, it must be some kind of centre where people rented office space.

She cut the engine and locked the car, then walked to the main door — more blue glass — on shaking legs. The nerves had kicked in, and she almost bolted, but she gripped the long, vertical steel handle and pushed her way inside into reception.

A woman sat behind the wide desk, only her shoulders and head visible it was so tall. Brunette, mid-thirties, pretty to the point it was obscene. Light-pink lipstick, smoky make-up around the eyes, a cream blouse open at the neck, a pendant sitting just above her ample cleavage.

"Hi. I'm Tracy Collier. I have an appointment with a therapist." *Shit. I've forgotten her name.*

"Which one?" the receptionist asked, smiling brightly with perfect teeth to go along with her perfect features.

Tracy looked for a badge or something to find out this woman's name and spotted a plaque on the desktop. KERRY. "I'm not sure, Kerry. Sorry."

"That's fine. I'll just run your name through the computer. One second." She tapped the keyboard with shiny black nail tips. "Ah, you're with Sasha Barrows. First floor, room seven."

"Thanks."

"I'll just let her know you've arrived. If you take the lift, her door is right beside it on your left."

"Thanks again."

While waiting for the lift to arrive, Tracy tapped her foot on the cream marble floor, her stomach doing a number on her. She needed the loo.

The lift came then, so she boarded and pressed the button with ONE on it. The smooth ride took seconds, and the doors opened silently onto a royal-blue carpeted hallway with a cream geometric design, the walls starling-wing black. She turned left and waited outside the teak door for a moment to remove herself from her scared little girl persona and into the detective version, hoping the blunt Tracy could carry her through her first session so she could get Sasha Barrows' measure and gauge whether she was the woman who could make the Past disappear. She'd done the same with Dr Fuckface.

She knocked.

"Come in."

This is it . . .

She opened the door, immediately setting her sights on Barrows sitting behind a black desk at the back in front of a huge sheet of window glass. Cerise blouse, dark-grey jacket. She assessed the woman's stoic appearance, sensed her no-nonsense air and, for fuck's sake, Tracy zipped straight back into vulnerable Collier, the young girl she'd been in the cupboard with the rainbow scarf over her eyes.

No. This isn't what's supposed to happen.

"Tracy?" Barrows asked.

Tracy nodded.

"Come on in and take a seat." Barrows rose, her skirt hem reaching her knees, and indicated a black leather chair beside a matching sofa. "Either place will do. Wherever you're comfortable."

Tracy closed the door and went for the chair — somewhere she could be alone, where Barrows couldn't sit next to her to offer comfort and a warm arm around her shoulder. Not that the therapist appeared the sort who would do that. And Tracy wouldn't allow it anyway. She could manage fine by herself, thank you, always had until Damon had come along — and even then, she was stubborn and preferred to be self-reliant. To deal with her hurts by herself.

"Would you like a tea or coffee?" Barrows asked. "Or I have some Coke if you're all right with sugary drinks."

"Coke please, that would be nice."

The therapist took off her jacket and draped it over her desk. Then, while Barrows went to a fridge set inside a cupboard, her feet bare — *what?* — Tracy thought about the woman's voice. Soft, it didn't match her somewhat hard-looking exterior. Barrows was all angles — jagged elbows, pointy knees, a chin and nose a witch would be proud of, minus the huge warts with hairs sprouting out of them.

You're such a bitch.

Barrows closed the fridge, and Tracy wondered why the therapist hadn't spoken again. Was that a tactic? To see if Tracy remained silent or talked nineteen to the dozen through nerves?

She decided she didn't care.

"There you go," Barrows said, handing Tracy a can and a glass.

Tracy chose not to use the latter. "Thank you. It's so hot today, isn't it?" *Pardon? Did I really just say that?* What had she become? Someone who blathered on about the weather as a conversation starter? *Help me . . .*

"Too hot. So, what can I help you with?" Straight to the point.

Like me. We'll get along fine. I hope.

Barrows sat on the sofa, in the farthest corner from Tracy, her top half kind of sprawled out as though she were at home. She tucked her legs up then opened her can. Her hair was so perfect, Tracy couldn't imagine it ever being mussed. She amused herself by thinking the woman slept with a hair net on to stop the waves tangling.

"I have issues," Tracy said. *Start as you mean to go on . . .* "I grew up abused, by my father, his friend, maybe others, I can't remember, and it screwed me up. I need you to unscrew me." She'd surprised herself at getting to the heart of the matter so quickly, a far cry from when she'd seen Fuckface.

When would she grow up and stop calling him that?

Now?

"I see. Have you talked to anyone about this before?" Barrows drank some Coke.

It prompted Tracy to open hers and take a swig. Barrows didn't swig, she daintily sipped, and Tracy felt like a lout in the presence of a princess.

"Yes. I had a session where a fair bit of the abuse came out, but unfortunately, my therapist was murdered, so we couldn't progress any further."

"Oh dear. Dr Schumer by any chance? I say that, because he's the only therapist I know in my circle who was killed."

"Yes, that's the one."

"Lovely man, if a bit warped at times. But he got the job done; amazing results with all his patients, so I heard. And me saying warped . . . They say don't talk ill of the dead, but he's *dead*, so what's he going to do?" She giggled and smiled, the kind conspirators shared.

Tracy relaxed a bit, but she had to make a point. "He didn't have a flawless track record. He was also my father's therapist, and he didn't fix him."

"Ah, we can't win them all, although we do try. What do you do for a living?"

"Police officer. I run the serious crimes squad."

"Like it?"

"For the most part."

"Why did you join up?"

"The cliché in all the crime books and TV shows — fucked-up girl needs something to keep her focused so she can right the wrongs done to her by helping those who need help."

"And here we have another cliché. Fucked-up policewoman visits therapist to help her come to terms with her fucked-up-ness."

Tracy raised her eyebrows at the fact Barrows swore. She hadn't expected that.

"And cliché or not, because this happens more than people realise," Barrows said, "you joining the force . . . it works, yes?"

"Yes. For now." *What does that even mean?*

"For now?"

"Things are . . . stressful at the moment. They have been since my father sent . . . a woman he knew to kill people to get my attention. To make sure I worked that case and realised it was him behind it all. He thought it would make me move back home. He was a dickhead like that."

"Sounds distressing. Was it?"

"Just a bit."

"And it's followed you around ever since, I take it?"

"Yes, the woman got away. She's still out there. Turns up every so often, to speak to me, to taunt me, knowing I won't do anything about her coming back for . . . reasons." It was harder to speak to Barrows about this than it had been with Schumer. He'd known exactly who and what her father had been, who Lisa was. This woman — she couldn't be told Lisa was her sister, that she was killing all over again. There was patient and client confidentiality, Schumer had banged on about that often enough, but Tracy didn't know whether Barrows took that kind of thing as seriously as he had, as in, not phoning the police to tell them her father was a paedophile and Lisa had been going around bumping people off for him. Barrows could decide to lift the phone as soon as Tracy left and spill everything.

"I can see why you need someone to talk to," Barrows said, resting her can on her knee and twisting it around and around. "It has to be hard to be a police officer when your father did what he did. There you are, supposed to uphold the law, and I'm guessing you were torn as to whether to arrest him. Were you?"

"Uh, no." Tracy blushed. *Tell the truth for once in your goddamned life.* "Yes."

"Why? Because he was your father and you had loyalty to deal with? Some sort of moral obligation?"

"No, because if I arrested him, the truth would come out." *I've been selfish to the core for as long as I can remember.*

"The truth?"

"About me. The abuse. I didn't want anyone to know."

"Ah, you poor thing. I would have wanted to kill him if that were me. Did you?"

"What, want to kill him, or did I kill him?"

"Either."

"I wanted to. I didn't." *But I wish I'd had that privilege.*

"Shame. You would have felt better if you had."

No, I wouldn't. I killed John, and I still don't feel better.

"Or not . . ." Barrows said. "So, where are you now? Where are you at in your head?"

"I need it all to go away. I've locked it all up — or so I thought — but things keep creeping out. Not the abuse — Dr Schumer helped me with that, and if there *are* other incidents and abusers I can't remember, I'd prefer not to at the moment. Although I do realise that the things I can't remember are probably still festering somewhere and need to come out eventually. What I need to deal with for now is me as a person. I have to find out whether the abuse and my upbringing made me how I am today or whether I'm just using that as an excuse to act the way I want and get away with it, especially with my partner, Damon. He's also my partner at work. I'm a bitch, quite frankly, and I don't like myself. My several selves."

"That's normal, you know, to have different versions of yourself. We all have them, some more than others. For example, there's the social self, where you become one type of person, all bubbly, the life and soul, and you act that out even when you don't want to. Then there's your reflective self, your judgmental self, your whatever self. There are so many. Some lucky people get away with just being two selves, but others . . . A self for every occasion, as it were."

"That's me. Sometimes I can be about four or five different versions in one day. It bothers me. I don't think that's normal, no matter what you say."

"It is. Which Tracy do you want to get rid of the most?"

"The bitch. The one who says things out loud that should stay in her head. The one who thinks bad things. The one who hurts people with what she says. The liar."

"Liar?"

"I tell lies all the time. To everyone, even myself. I have to, to hide what I've done."

"Which is?"

"I'm not prepared to talk about that."

"Perhaps not yet."

"No, seriously, I can't talk about that. To anyone. Not even you." *Only to Lisa, who knows everything.*

"Okay. So how do you propose to get rid of the Bitchy Tracy? Have you tried?"

"Yes. Damon has helped. He grounds me, points out when I've gone overboard, but at the same time I know he loves me — each one of me, he's said so. I don't know who I'd be now if I didn't have him. Some extremely bitter cow, I think. Or more bitter, anyway, because I'm already a bitter cow."

"Do you want to know what I believe?"

"Go on." *Schumer did this. Analysed me. Is it in their training to guess who you are based on a few minutes?*

"That you're a wonderful human beneath all the layers, you just can't let yourself become her because you don't feel you deserve it. You've been told somewhere down the line that you're worthless — around the time you were solely the Tracy you want to be again, a child, an innocent, and in order to cope with the loss of that part of yourself, you created more sides — sides who can cope better — and eventually, the real you got lost, buried beneath not only the weight of your other selves, but the burdens you were forced to carry. *Are* forced to carry."

Tears ran down Tracy's cheeks. Hot. Surprising. She didn't cry. Not anymore, yet here she was . . .

Shit.

"What you need to understand, Tracy, is that you are a product of someone else's making. Their actions meant you became who you are to protect yourself. If it wasn't for them, you wouldn't have had to become these other versions. You are not at fault. It's inbuilt in us to survive the best way we can despite the circumstances, and yours, which were undoubtedly extreme, meant *you* had to be extreme in building personas who enabled you to cope. With your father gone, those barriers should have crumbled, perhaps disappeared by now, or at least be tucked away in your head somewhere, forgotten. But they haven't, so there is either something going on where you still need that protection, or you've become so used to being who you currently are, you're afraid to let her go because she's kept you safe for so long."

A lump formed in Tracy's throat. She tried to swallow it. Couldn't.

"Tracy, what was done to you isn't who you are. It's a part of you, yes, something that's shaped you, but it doesn't define you. Your real self is in there somewhere, that trusting, innocent person, and you can find her again — *if* you allow yourself to do so. Breaking the pattern of your other sides coming out from your habit of relying on them *can* be done, and I will help you to do that."

A sob barked out of Tracy, and she didn't even raise her hand as she usually would to hide her ugly-cry mouth.

"Would you like a cuddle, Tracy?"

She stared at Barrows through the mist of tears.

And nodded.

CHAPTER TWENTY

It's my usual night off, and I've caught up on all the sleep I lost over the Mrs Roberts thing. I phoned Zello earlier to ask if she really did blame me for what had happened — it'd been playing on my mind, see. I needed the truth — or the truth as she saw it anyway. I'd entertained thoughts of her poisoning everyone's minds, getting them to think it was my fault, and imagined going back to work and having no one speaking to me.

I don't want that to happen again. It's lonely when no one except your mother talks to you.

My childhood was spent with no friends once Mother pulled me out of school and decided to teach me herself. Once she died, I became a different version of me and went to college, university, then trained to be a nurse. Now I'm working at Blooming Age, it means I have some friends. All right, we don't meet up after hours for coffee or anything, or ring each other, go clothes shopping and whatnot, but we get along fine — Nurse Matthews is my favourite — and I can pretend I'm part of the gang, even though I'm not really. I've never fitted in anywhere, so I'd be kidding myself if I thought I could in the proper sense. I'm the loner, the outcast, still walking around with those name tags attached, but it isn't as obvious as before.

I've learnt to hide behind a facade.

"No, Chrissy, I don't blame you," Zello had said. "I've decided it's a joint responsibility thing, me included. I've had time to think about it — that Collier woman sowed some rather spiteful seeds, making me take a good long look at myself and my role in this . . . this awful thing. But she was right to do so, even if what she implied hurt me somewhat. *Everyone* fell asleep, not just you. Plus, I've realised your hours are ridiculous. I've spoken to the owner, and we're going to restructure working times so all the night staff get more of a break between shifts. When you think about it, you have a weekend of being zonked out most of Saturday. Sunday you get up at a normal time, then you're back in for a twelve-hour stint that night, effectively losing eight hours of sleep. It messes with the body clock, so no wonder you all dropped off."

I hadn't expected her to be so understanding. "But will my hours be less? Won't that alter my pay?"

"This is what we need to look into. We don't want to reduce wages, not when you've all got used to what you earn and have bills to pay."

Relief had all but knocked me off my damn feet. Okay, I don't have a mortgage or rent to fork out for, but the electricity bill is high, what with this place being so big. Old Victorian efforts tend to have heat seeping through gaps in the window frames.

I should sell this house really.

I sigh and rub my palms over my face, and that knocking comes again. It's occasionally during the day when I'm actually here, but mainly in the evenings before I start work, or in the middle of the night when I'm not at Blooming Age, and it wakes me up whenever it happens. It's as though the rats doze all day and only venture out when it gets dark. I don't want to go down there and see what it is, but if I don't, the rats could be doing all sorts of damage, couldn't they?

I take a deep breath and unlock the cellar door with the dull-grey key that used to be slightly shinier when I was a kid. The end poking out of the keeper is intricate filigree; maybe the key is an original from all those years ago. It'd stuck a bit when I'd twisted it just now — rust most likely — and I think about getting a new one cut, although there really isn't any need. I don't like going down there and avoid it as much as possible, but it seems I have to go now.

God . . .

I swing the door wide, and a revolting smell wafts out — piss, shit, mustiness, possibly damp and mould — and the former two remind me of work when the oldies have accidents. I pinch my nose and venture down, the cement stairs cold on my bare feet, and at the bottom, I stand still and listen. The light from the hallway above doesn't reach this far, the shaft at the top bright, fading with each step until it bleeds into the darkness and becomes one with it. I strain my ears for signs of rats scurrying, trying to find a way out having sensed I'm here. But there's no *shushing* of little pink paw pads and the scrape of gnarly claws on the floor, no swish of tails brushing it, nothing except . . .

Breathing.

My stomach churns, and I suck air in, my mind spinning. Are the rats so big I'd pick up on something like their breaths? I've heard they can be as large as cats, but even so . . .

It comes again, that breathing, quick, uneven, like I'd sounded as a child when frightened. I need to turn the light on, to see what's making that noise, but I'm scared of rats. Should I call the environmental health department and let them deal with it?

No.

So I don't talk myself out of it, I flick the switch on the wall beside me, and the room floods with light while my body overflows with dread. In the corner isn't a rat. It isn't a cat-sized lump of vermin that's been knocking into the furniture like I'd thought. It's a woman, a skinny woman, dirty, her face streaked with God knows what — *it can't be shit, can it?* — a filthy rag tied around the lower half of her face, between her pale, chapped lips. Her wide eyes fill with tears, and she snorts from her nose, snot flying, and the exhalation doesn't even shift the greasy black hair hanging over her cheeks in strands.

What on earth is she doing here?

I glance at the table in the middle, the one I used to sit at before Mother died and I stored it. There's a few syringes and some small bottles of clear fluid. I recognise the labels on the medication — it helps people to sleep. Mother's old stuff? Why didn't I put that away? *Throw* it away?

Reluctantly, I turn my attention to the thing in the corner. "How . . . how did you get in?" I can't get over this. I can see her, she's definitely there, but my mind doesn't want to process it.

She lifts her hands, and the wrists are bound with those cable ties, like the ones I bought a while back to hold the stems of my wooden flower arrangement in place. They're the same colour, too, bright yellow, and I frown, trying to work out *why* she's here, why those ties are here, why her ankles are held together with them.

And why she's naked.

I want to take the gag off her, but she looks feral. What if she bites me? Lashes out if I cut those ties off?

Should I call the police or what?

No.

My forehead hurts from frowning, and I stare at her. She stares back then flits her eyes to the side, like she's trying to tell me something. Oh God, is someone else with us? Someone in the other corner? The person who put this woman here?

I don't want to look. I want to run upstairs, lock the door, and forget I ever saw her. But what if she dies? She'll smell after a while, and the neighbours will come round, asking if my waste pipes are blocked, and they might call someone in, and this . . . this person will be discovered, and I'll get the blame, like I did at first over Mrs Roberts.

This isn't my fault. This isn't anything to do with me.

Fear scuttles up my spine, and it morphs into what I imagine is an entity that roves its ghostly hands over my skin, bringing out goosebumps and the need to cry and cry and cry until all my tears are gone.

She whimpers, that huddle of skin-and-bone scruff, and snaps her head to where she'd been silently asking me to look.

Don't make me do this.

My heart hurts, pounds so hard, my pulse womb-sounding in my ears, and I feel sick, so damn sick. Bile rears its bitter-tasting head, and I swallow it, clutching my stomach as if that will stop my dinner coming back up.

And I turn my head.

Women stand there — *oh my god . . . what the fucking hell . . . who are they?* — but they don't seem right. It's like they're distorted, and I blink, thinking it's my eyes playing tricks on me. It isn't. There they are, faces skewed, eyes bulging, skin sagging in places — on the cheeks and chin — and they're watching me, standing stock still, staring, staring, staring.

"Who? What . . . ?" My voice isn't mine. It belongs to the child I once was, hoarse from all the crying I used to do, broken and jagged, hitching on a sob. The urge to run is strong, fight or flight overcoming me, but my feet won't move. I gawp at the tied-up woman then, unable to stand looking at the other two any longer. I ask her with my eyes: *What's going on? Who are you all? Why are you all here?*

She doesn't answer — can't, can she? — and gazes back at me with what I think is pleading: Help me.

No.

I back up to the bottom of the stairs, slap at the light switch, the darkness erasing everything from sight but not from my mind. No, not from there — it's seared into my brain, something I'll never forget, and panic takes over, sending me breathless. I scrabble up and burst out into the bright hallway and clutch my chest, struggling to lock the door. The fucking key is sticking again, and my shaking hand doesn't help.

"Lock, damn you. Lock."

It does, and I press my back to the door, snapping my eyes shut, tight, so tight, willing my breathing to calm the hell down.

What do I do? I can't leave them all down there. That's a crime, keeping people against their will. Who put them there? *Why* are they there?

I don't know, I don't bloody know, but blackness creeps into the edges of my vision, and I know I'm going to faint. I can't stop it, even by talking to myself, telling the me who is full of fear that I must remain awake, and I slide down the door, closing my eyes, my mind mercifully going blank.

CHAPTER TWENTY-ONE

The Past

"What the hell have you done?" Mother screams at Father.

She stalks across the room and flaps an envelope in Father's face. Hers is flushed, and she looks ever so angry. Angry enough to hurt someone.

They don't notice him. He cowers in the corner — it's best he keeps out of their way when they're like this. They always fight, or it seems so anyway. He needs a wee but doesn't dare get up. That means he'll have to walk past them, and she'll notice, his mother, and bring him into the argument: "Tell your dad what came in the post today. That thing I showed you," that's what she'll say. And he doesn't want her to. Doesn't want to hear those words.

"I haven't done anything," Father says, and bright spots of colour slink onto his cheeks, and that always means he's lying.

"You've been at it again, haven't you?" Mother waves the envelope even more; it crackles with each flutter.

He knows what's inside, and it hurts, that knowledge. Isn't he enough? Isn't his mother enough for his father?

"You opened my mail?" Father stares, his eyes wide, his jaw dropping. A big bubble of spit grows at the corner of his mouth, and it pops, coating his skin in a glistening sheen. "You said you wouldn't do that again."

"And you said you wouldn't do certain things again, yet you did them anyway. You've been acting funny lately, like you did before with that bitch, and I told you back then: one more time, and we're finished. Over. And it seems you've done it regardless; otherwise, why the letter? Why would she be sending you messages through a solicitor to leave her alone if you haven't been doing anything?"

"Shit." Father rubs a hand over his face, but he's peeping through the gap between two fingers.

"I can see you," Mother says. "Staring at me. Hiding your face won't make the crime go away."

"Crime?" Father lowers his hand and frowns.

"It's a crime to have sex with someone while you're married," she says, folding her arms over her belly.

"No, it isn't," he says. "It really isn't."

"Oh, so you've looked it up have you, in one of your encyclopaedias that cost a damn fortune — a fortune we couldn't afford at the time? Or have you asked around, let other people twig what you've been up to? My God, you're something else, you are." She opens the envelope, pulls out the letter, and reads in silence. Then, "Listen to the wording this fella here has put about adultery. 'Physical contact with an alien and unlawful organ'." She laughs, and it sounds bitter, her face screwed up as if she's eaten something sour. "Unlawful. You hear that? The organ, the alien — called Irene, let's not forget that — is unlawful."

"Stop it," Father says. "And give me that." He snatches the letter, scanning it, his face going redder by the second. "Shit."

"Yes. Shit. That's what you are, a huge piece of it. So tell me, is she worth it? She's married — you see that? Irene Roberts she's called now. Don't you think you ought to stay away from her? It's clear she listened to my warning all those years ago. A slap or two helps and all. She's getting on with her life, unlike you. Oh, and we mustn't overlook what else it says in the letter. That you've told her you're coming to get her, that you'll send other people after her if she doesn't do what you want. And that, I presume, is running away with you."

"Mind your own business," Father says.

Mother gapes at him. "I beg your pardon?"

"Nothing." Father crumples the letter and slings the ball of paper into the open fire.

It crackles and spits and growls, the flames licking upwards, as though the tips are trying to escape up the chimney, away from the tension.

From the safety of the corner, he scrunches himself into a ball just like that letter and wishes his parents would be quiet, be like a normal family, same as the ones on TV. He stares at the fire, the sudden urge to throw himself on it taking over, and he shivers, afraid and confused at his feelings.

Father and Mother shout at each other, but he's tuned them out. He can't listen anymore. There's the sound of a door slamming, and it snaps him out of his trance. He looks at Mother, who rushes over and yanks him up by the collar of his shirt, dragging him into the kitchen.

She sits him down at the table and tells him how wicked Irene Roberts is, how wicked Father is, and that they must be stopped, the pair of them. Then she outlines a plan, saying, "When your father is gone, I'll be the one telling Irene fucking Roberts that people are coming to get her, and when I'm gone, too, you'll take over."

Every day of his life for the next few years, she repeats it, goes over it, until it's branded into his mind and becomes all he can think of.

Mrs Roberts is a bad lady.

Mrs Roberts has to die.

CHAPTER TWENTY-TWO

He sits in the taxi a few houses down from the green door, on the other side of the road, and waits. It's six thirty, and he thinks she'll come out in a minute, to go off then stroll along Jester Street, ready to tout for business.

Zello didn't call him in on his night off to make up for the extra shift he'd missed because of Mrs Roberts. If that stupid cow hadn't turned up at the care home, she'd still be alive. He'd got over it, over *her*, had taught himself some mindfulness activities, and it meant he'd forgotten about her, becoming the man who didn't wear the trousers, the shirt, and the taupe tie — becoming this self, the one he is now — again — just because Mrs Roberts had grown old and needed care.

She always was such a selfish bitch. Always took what she wanted without a second thought. Well, she can't think at all now, can she, and he hopes her soul is rotting in Hell while her body is stone cold in the morgue fridge. Cold like her actions back then.

Dirty Girl opens the green door, steps outside, and closes it behind her. She totters to the kerb and sticks a key in the lock of an older model car. What? She owns a vehicle? He wasn't expecting that at all, and the thought flits through his mind that she must park up in town then go on foot to Jester Street. It's a sensible thing to do, what with men out there willing to kill prostitutes — *it should be funny, but it fucking isn't* — but this has messed with his plans.

He was going to follow her in his car, slow, while she walked, until she turned the corner into an alley that leads to the high street, then nab her there, but now?

You absolute bitch.

She gets in the driver's seat, and her headlights splash into the darkness. Can she see him across the street? Is he now visible as a silhouette inside the taxi, a greyed-out shape that'll put her on alert?

Fuckfuckfuck.

He slams the heel of his hand on the steering wheel, and the horn blares. While he curses himself for his stupidity in allowing anger to take over, and stares over at *her* silhouette, he shakes his head and raises his hands as if to say: What a dumb sod I am, eh?

Her shoulders lift, as if she's shrugging, thinking nothing of what just happened, already relegating it to a file in her mind labelled INSIGNIFICANT. She backs up a bit, then oozes out of her parking space to drive right past him, not looking out of the passenger-side window. He has to be quick if he's going to keep up with her and swears at himself yet again for parking this way round. She would have walked in the direction she's now gone, so why didn't he think of that?

There's too much on his mind. Too much going on.

Why couldn't life have stayed as it was those ten years before Mrs Roberts had come along? Why did everything have to go so wrong?

He turns the car and manages to catch up to her, his front bumper inches from her rear one. Coaching himself calm, he backs off a little — he can't be doing with her catching on to him tailing her. For all he knows, she could have clocked that he drives a taxi, back there when he'd hit the horn, so to see one right up her arse now isn't what he needs.

She drives to the multistorey car park, finds an empty spot on the lowest level, and gets out. No one else is around, so he swerves in beside her, leaps out as she's turning the key to lock up, and punches her on the back of the head. Her keys go flying, landing with a clatter. She doesn't have a chance to fight back. She surges forward from another punch he wallops her with, forehead smacking into the driver's-side window, and he hits her again and again, until she's subdued and dazed enough that he can bundle her into the boot of the taxi and zoom away.

Cameras. There's bound to have been cameras in there.

That's something he'll have to think about later. He'll decide what to do then. But he isn't dressed in his usual clothing, and he looks nothing like who he really is, the person deep inside who doesn't want to hurt anyone, doesn't want to remember his childhood, doesn't want to remember all the things he does, so if he's seen on any CCTV, what does it matter?

The taxi may pose a bit of a problem, though. Again, thoughts for another time.

He travels through the streets at a sedate pace, not wanting to draw attention to himself. The light on the roof of the taxi is out, and he looks for all the world like a cabbie on his way home after a long shift.

In his street, he glances around, ensuring no one can see him. Then he parks on the drive, gets out to open the garage door, then he's back in the car, easing it inside. Engine and headlights off, he takes a moment, sitting in the darkness, to think about what just happened. Mother always said that if the plan deviates, things unravel. Things go wrong.

He can only hope she isn't right this time.

Sucking in a long, soul-soothing breath, he exits the car, shuts the garage, and opens the boot. The little interior light comes on in the top-right corner, concentrated on her head and the tangled hair on it.

He frowns.

He lifts Dirty Girl out, and she groans, one arm wedged between them, the other dangling. She lifts that one and rubs her forehead, then her scalp, probably trying to ease the pain he'd inflicted. There's a whole lot more pain in her future, but once she's gone, he has nothing to worry about. There's no one she can tell about what he made her do at Blooming Age. What he did to Mrs Roberts in that field. It seems ages ago now, as though it happened in another lifetime.

What if she's already told someone what happened?

He flicks that annoying thought to the back of his mind and carries her into the house, recalling, for some bizarre reason, when this garage had been added to the property. His father had employed builders, and the new construction had sprouted up between this house and the one next door, and it hadn't been long before the neighbour had done the same. These two houses had been the only ones with driveways between them. The rest are terraced, so only one neighbour is joined to him, and they won't hear anything anyway. Seems they're out.

While he takes her down into the basement, he recalls playing in the driveways with his skipping rope, before the garages had been built, before he'd been forced to become who he is now, when he'd worn other clothes more suited to who he truly is.

He drops her on the floor, and she cries out. He switches on the light. Stares at the bitch in the corner, who has hope in her eyes, which quickly douses upon seeing him. Who had she expected other than him? Maybe the silly cow is delirious with hunger.

"You can help me this time," he says, "instead of sitting there watching like a useless piece of shit."

She sniffs in a breath, and he wonders if she's imagining skinning Dirty Girl with him, just like he'd done in front of her with his latest acquisition in the other corner. No. He wouldn't trust her with a fleshing knife — or any knife for that matter. It would end up plunged into his gut, his face, his heart.

"You can kill her for me. That'll teach you, won't it, Irene?"

She narrows her eyes in confusion, and he has no idea why. Doesn't she remember her own name?

"You can suffocate her," he says. "That won't take much energy, tying a bag over her head. You'll be weaker than I'd like. I forgot to feed you, didn't I?"

Irene whimpers and nods, and Dirty Girl seems to come alive at the sound, snapping her head up and pushing on her hands so her torso is off the floor.

"Irene?" Dirty Girl whispers. "But she's dead . . . She's old . . ."

"Shut up." He kicks Dirty Girl in the stomach.

She lets out an *oomph* and rolls onto her back, clutching her midsection and crying.

Noise. It hurts his head.

"Stop that!" he snaps.

Dirty Girl laughs, bordering on hysterical, and he stares at her. What the hell set her off?

"Oh God," Dirty Girl says, more burbles coming out of her wide mouth. "To think it's going to end like this. I thought . . . I thought it would be somewhere else, at the hands of someone else."

"What the fuck are you on about?" he says, getting hacked off at her babbling.

"Oh, knob off, you," she says, sounding weary of him, like he doesn't matter, is of no consequence.

His anger level rises. She's supposed to be frightened of him, not laughing. He kicks her again, but she only cackles louder.

"You," he says, pointing to Irene. "You're going to shut her up."

Irene shakes her head, and he bends over to haul Dirty Girl to her feet, shoving her against the wall so her head smacks into it. She glares at him, defiance and maybe a hint of madness in her shining irises, and he has to look away, the freckles on her cheeks dancing in his mind's eye. Why hadn't he noticed them before? If he had, he'd never have chosen her. Mrs Roberts hadn't had any.

Shit.

"What's the matter?" Dirty Girl asks. "Lost your bottle?" She smiles. "It's easy, you know, killing, although I reckon *being* killed isn't. Want to find out?"

What is this? Reverse psychology? He isn't having any of it, isn't allowing her to derail his plans. She's going to die, and that's the end of it. No pissing about.

He drags her to the table in the middle, forcing her to bend so her front is flush against the top. Syringes and small bottles skitter off and land on the floor. It sounds like one of the medicines have broken. He reaches into the drawer beneath for cable ties, the bright yellow of them glaring, too much for his frazzled nerves. He binds her wrists behind her, then grips her hair and slams her face down. A satisfying crack, a pained growl, and blood splattering onto the wood.

That's her nose fucked.

He smiles, more in control now, and secures her ankles together. Then he whips her over onto her back and stares at the new freckles on her cheeks, only they're red and not brown.

"Do *you* want to find out?" he asks, "what it's like to be killed?"

She grins, her teeth claret covered. "I do." Her eyes gleam even more. "I fucking do. Go on, do it. Kill me. Make all this shit go away — all the lies, the deceit, the bastard fear."

He frowns, unsure what to say to that. She's meant to fight it, to be afraid of death.

"I'm tired of it all," she says. "Of everything."

"Shut your fucking face," he says, sensing the control slipping from him to Dirty Girl. This wasn't how it was meant to go, her taking the reins, orchestrating events. He roughly manhandles her to a chair at the other end of the table and presses her into it. "You're going to sit there and shut the hell up." Then he stuffs a rag into her mouth.

The bitch laughs again, the gurgles muffled.

She's insane, got to be.

"Now you," he says, grabbing scissors from the table drawer and going over to Irene. He snips the cable ties and lifts her to her feet. "You're going to do exactly what I said. That bag over there." He jerks his head at a plastic carrier hanging from a hook on the wall by Mother and her crones. "Empty the contents out and put the bag over this bitch's head."

Irene hobbles as though she hasn't walked for months, and he almost laughs along with Dirty Girl, who is still letting out an irritating racket. Irene takes the bag down and shuffles to the table, wincing, tears falling, and pours the things out. Several glass eyeballs roll over the wooden surface, a few onto the floor, and Irene squeals, jumping back as much as she's able in her condition.

Shit stains her legs.

Dear God . . .

"Do it," he says. "Put that bag over her head and pull it tight around her neck."

She does as she's told, sobbing, sniffing, and while Dirty Girl just sits there and lets it happen, as though she'd meant what she'd said, and she's truly had enough, he shoves her hair inside then secures a long cable tie around her neck, pulling the strap tight.

"And now we stand and watch her suffer," he says, "for what the likes of her do to people like me and Mother."

He stares, transfixed as Dirty Girl breathes, and the bag flattens to the contours of her face, then billows out as she exhales. The fascinating motions repeat, repeat, repeat until the bag is sucked to her face and doesn't release again. Despite claiming she wants to die, once there's no more air, Dirty Girl struggles. She brings her hands up to the cable tie, fingers scrabbling to gain purchase, and her body writhes. Then she falls off the chair, slapping onto the floor, and he's unable to take his attention off her.

She's dying, without him having to do a thing — he's not to blame for this one.

Irene is.

Irene.

He spins, glancing around — there's Mother, there's the fake Mrs Roberts, and the new bitch makes three, but Irene isn't there with them or in her corner. He spins again, and she advances on him, the scissors he'd used to clip her cable ties raised above her head, the point aiming straight for him.

CHAPTER TWENTY-THREE

Tracy had stayed with Barrows for longer than her time slot, the therapist saying Tracy was her last patient and she didn't have anything to rush home for. They'd nattered for ages, Tracy actually comfortable for once, the same as she was when chatting with Damon, or when she'd been proper friends with her old mate Kathy.

It didn't make sense, was alien, but she liked it.

"Therapists also fuck up in life," Barrows said now. "I'm divorced. No kids. Married to my job and patients. Apparently, I care more for them than I did my ex-husband, and now I look back on it, he was right." Barrows shrugged and smiled, although it was a sad one.

"Glad to know it isn't just me who's a fuck-up," Tracy said. "I'm beginning to wonder whether I'll ever be free of this shit. At the moment, it's all my fears getting to me — fear of what might happen if . . . Well, that subject is what I told you I won't talk about."

"It'll come out eventually, you know." Barrows sipped her coffee — they'd switched from Coke an hour ago, and it was coming up to seven thirty.

After this cup, Tracy would have to get going. She couldn't sit here all night, much as she wanted to — which was strange, considering she didn't 'do' friends and had a job to finish at the station. Still, Damon would ring if he'd found anything. She'd texted him at the official end of her session and let him know she'd be stopping on for a bit. Guilt was chewing on her nerves now, though, at the thought of him working away while she chilled out. She was pleased to feel that guilt. Like Barrows had said earlier, if Tracy felt guilt, it meant she wasn't a complete psychopath, maybe just three-quarters narcissist.

Tracy had laughed at that. Oddly, the remark hadn't upset or rankled her.

Barrows was good for her soul, it seemed.

"What makes you say I'll spill it all to you eventually?" Tracy asked.

"I can tell. The things you've already told me — in and out of the session — isn't usual for a first appointment. Most people who have big things to hide, like you do, well, they don't divulge much at first. Too busy worrying about whether they'll slip up and blurt something out. But you? You've had years to perfect the art of not allowing secrets to pop out, so you feel safe to natter to me."

"That sounds awful," Tracy said. "'Perfect the art'. I've basically been lying since I was a child."

"Out of necessity, remember."

Tracy nodded. And she *would* remember that. During the Collier case, she'd repeatedly told herself she wasn't to blame for her childhood, that it wasn't her fault her whacko father had totally lost the fucking plot, the pages, and even the actual book cover, and since forever she'd made sure she didn't allow anyone to point the finger at her and say something was her doing when it wasn't.

It had become a bit of an obsession, but it was time to let that go. To let lots of things go. Already she felt better, actually seeing the light at the end of a previously long tunnel, but Lisa was still there in the shadows somewhere, pressed against the brickwork, the Pied Piper, playing her tune, and Tracy the rat, dancing to it.

Without using Lisa's name and revealing she was her sibling, Tracy explained that metaphor to Barrows.

"So, steal her flute or whatever the hell the Pied Piper used," Barrows said.

"It's not as easy as that. If I could tell you, you'd understand, but I can't."

Barrows nodded, and Tracy finished her drink. She stood and took the cup over to Barrows' desk and placed it on the blotter.

"Bill me for the extra time, won't you?" Tracy asked, walking towards the sofa. She held out a hand and shook Barrows'. "And thank you for this evening. You've helped a great deal. Sorry about the tears and the overly long hug."

Barrows rose, not bothering to straighten her ruched skirt or smooth her top. "One, I'm absolutely not billing you for the extra. That was girlie time, something I don't get much of, and I appreciate being able to kick back. Two, don't be sorry for crying. You needed to. Bottle things up too long, and the cork bursts out, the contents inside spilling. And as for the hug, I kind of needed one myself, so I was selfish and grabbed it while I could." She winked.

"You're a shit liar."

"I know. Worth a try, though."

Tracy laughed, and it felt so bloody good. "I really have to go. Middle of a case and all that. It won't be long before it hits the news, and you'll hear all about it."

"Good luck with it." Barrows moved to the door and grasped the handle. "Same time next week? Maybe, if you can stay on again, we'll have a tipple instead of coffee."

"Maybe. If this case isn't wrapped up, I might not be able to make it, but I'll give the receptionist a bell if that happens."

"A day's notice at least, if you can. Otherwise you get billed anyway. It's better if I can offer the slot to someone else who needs it." Barrows opened the door. "See you soon. And remember—"

"I know, I know: it's not my fault. Catch you next week. And thanks again."

Tracy left and stood in front of the lift, pressing the button and waiting for it to arrive. Once it did, she stepped on, reluctantly switching her mind from the lovely time she'd just had to Lisa. The lift landed, and she strode out into the reception area. Kerry had gone, and in her place behind the desk sat a male security guard. He got up and walked towards the main door, sliding the long chain dangling from his belt through his fingers then holding the bunch of keys at the end.

He tilted his head at her, a questioning gesture, so she flashed her warrant card. His eyes bulged, and he unlocked the door, swinging it open to allow her to leave. She breezed through, and in her car she sat for a few seconds to release a sigh, imagining it carried her worries along with it. Or some of them anyway. She'd known for a long time what needed to be done, had even thought about it a couple of times recently, but to *actually contemplate* doing it . . .

Killing Lisa would take planning, and while Tracy knew all the tricks to stop evidence from her body dropping at a scene, she couldn't do anything about the minute particles transferring onto her, then in her car, and in her home, tainting Damon's safe place without him even knowing it.

Could she do that?

She'd been lucky with John. She had happened to be at the scene for her job, so killing him had been something she'd got away with and blamed on Lisa. Everyone had swallowed the story, and if Lisa wasn't still skulking around, that barrel of bullshit would be well and truly over by now, forgotten.

But Lisa hadn't stayed away as she'd promised, and things had turned to crap. So Tracy would just have to use a giant pooper scooper and clean it up, wouldn't she.

She gunned the engine and set off, her mind on how she'd lure Lisa to meet her, the location, and method of murder. She didn't feel bad about those thoughts either. Maybe the apple didn't fall so far from the tree after all. Her father had killed, as had his two daughters.

What an absolute nightmare this had all ended up being.

She arrived at the station in good time, having missed the rush hour traffic, and waved at the night-desk sergeant on her way towards the stairs. She legged it up the three flights and bounded into the incident room, out of breath, full of energy and new purpose.

Damon turned in his chair, the castors squeaking. "Did it really go okay?" His expression was full of worry, despite her telling him in a text it had gone fine.

She kissed his forehead. "Of course it did. Do you think I'd have stayed on for longer if it hadn't? She's bloody brilliant, and I'll be right as rain in no time. You won't recognise the person I really am underneath when she comes crawling out of the hole she's been hiding in." She smiled.

"Bloody hell, you already seem different. What, did she give you some sort of medication in a drink or something?" He stood and brought her close, his hands on her backside.

"Oi, no touching the boss at work."

"It's outside hours."

"We're on overtime."

He raised his eyebrows. "Uh, *I'm* on overtime, you mean."

She slapped his chest and laughed. "Seriously now, it was great, and if she'll take you on, if it isn't a conflict or interest or whatever, you'll do well with her. If not, she'll know someone else you can see." She huffed out a breath, loath to change the subject, but she had to. "Did you find anything out while I was gone?"

"I did. Didn't you get my text?"

She frowned. Got her phone out of her pocket. A message envelope sat at the top of the screen. "Shit, must have been miles away on the ride here." *That's an understatement.* She shoved her phone away.

"It was lucky you turned up when you did, because I was about to ring Winter and tell him where I was going, picking Alastair up on the way as backup."

"Seriously? You have a name and address?" The hair prickled on the back of her neck, and her stomach flipped over. "From the taxi search?"

"Yes. I got nothing whatsoever from ex-taxi sales so had another look at the CCTV we were going to check again tomorrow. The last taxi we couldn't identify, because the licence plate was partially obscured, just happened to have an obvious Mondeo look to it, so I plugged in that make, all the dark colours, and the G-nine-three visible on the plate. That narrowed it down to only fourteen vehicles, surprisingly, with variations of the G-nine-three. I thought it was too good to be true, to be honest, but one of the vehicles is registered in this town with the complete G-nine-three in sequence. The other thirteen are elsewhere in the country."

"Christ. We could have done this much earlier and saved a heap of time." *Don't beat yourself up.* "Can we *really* have got that lucky so soon, though?" Dare she hope it would be over in a matter of hours? "Where is it registered?"

"Same street as one of the nurses from Blooming Age."

"Fucking hell . . . Is this turning into the Robin's Way saga all over again? And what's their name?"

"A Mr Simon Cowell."

"What?" She barked out laughter. "That's got to be some kind of sodding joke, right?"

"I know. If he's not our man, we can at least have him for impersonating someone else if he isn't really who he says he is, so it won't be a complete waste of time. Come on."

They left the incident room, and at the desk downstairs, Damon told the sergeant where they'd be.

"We'll phone in if we need backup," Tracy said. She didn't want any until she knew what and who they were dealing with. This Simon fella might well just be an innocent person who'd bought the taxi and could provide an alibi for the night in question.

In the car, they didn't talk, and Tracy tried to remember which nurse lived in that street. She didn't ask Damon for clarification through embarrassment. She couldn't admit she'd forgotten, her head being so stuffed with too many things, more than the average person probably had in theirs, like bundles of lies and suitcases full of bullshit.

They arrived, and although the street was familiar, she still couldn't recall the nurse. They'd visited so many, and she consoled herself with that fact.

"Just here," Damon said, pointing out of the window.

They got out, and Tracy waited on the path so Damon could peer through the ground floor front window, which was in darkness, although a faint line of light low down in the unlit hallway beyond the clear glass in the front door announced itself as a gap beneath another door. She pointed, and Damon nodded.

"Someone might be in," she said and knocked on the glass.

The door inside opened, revealing a man with a backdrop of creamy light, a kitchen sink unit behind him. His blue checked pyjama bottoms and a white vest had Tracy longing to get into her own nightwear and slip into bed. He walked towards them, frowning, appearing half asleep, as though he was ready for an early night.

He opened the front door and gave a tentative smile.

"Simon Cowell?" Tracy asked.

He looked upwards, as though he waited for some quip or other to follow, then stared directly at her. "No, Simon Cowdell."

"I see." Tracy smiled back. "Only, your licence details say Cowell."

"They bloody don't," he said. "And who are you anyway, coming here asking shit like that?"

Fuck.

"Sorry. I'm DI Tracy Collier, and this is DS Damon Hanks. Can we have a look at your licence, please?"

"Why? I haven't had notification of any speeding tickets or anything."

"Please?" Tracy cocked her head, and Damon stepped closer to her, presenting a united front.

"Hang on." Cowdell stomped off into the room at the front, and a light came on.

Tracy eased back to look inside through the window — a living room, half a black sofa visible, and a Gustav Klimt print of some naked blonde woman with flowers dotted around her.

Cowdell returned and held out his licence. "Well, fuck me, I never noticed it said Cowell before. I'll have to get that changed. Got to be someone at DVLA having a bloody laugh."

Tracy leant towards him and gave it the once-over. "Do you own a taxi? Mondeo?"

"Nope. Grey Ford Focus. Want the registration certificate?"

"If you don't mind." Tracy smiled again. *Why isn't he asking us inside? Is he who we're after?* She steeled herself for him coming back with a weapon, cursing for not insisting they put stab vests on before they'd left the station.

"Don't," Damon whispered. "I just thought the same thing."

"What?" she said, testing their connection.

"Vests."

Goosebumps sprang up on her arms that he'd guessed her thoughts. "Creepy bastard." She laughed unsteadily.

Cowdell reappeared. "Here you go. And it's that vehicle there, look." He nodded behind them.

Tracy didn't turn to see it. If she and Damon both did that, Cowdell could strike while their backs were turned. She stared at Cowdell, who frowned as though thinking.

"But if it's a taxi you're after, I'm sure I saw one going into the garage of a house a few doors down earlier," he said.

"Which one?" Tracy asked, her heart rate kicking into overdrive.

A scream pierced her ears, and she shot her attention in the direction it had come from. A naked woman stood on a doorstep two houses away to the left, then streaked through the garden and out onto the pavement, heading their way.

Damon dashed to intercept her, and Tracy followed, widening her eyes at the state of her. She had dried shit on her legs, her hair was filthy, as was her face, and blood spatter coated her breasts and stomach, drips of it striping her arms.

"That one!" Cowdell shouted. "That house she just came out of."

Tracy ignored him, holding her hands out to the woman. "It's all right, we're police officers. You're safe now." *Or you'll be arrested, depending on what you've done to get that blood on you.*

Damon slowly brought out his ID and showed it to the shaking state in front of them. "I'm going to give you my jacket, all right?" he said, removing it then taking a step towards her.

She raised her hands and shook her head. "Don't hurt me. Please, don't hurt me." Painfully thin, she appeared half starved and on the verge of collapsing.

Damon placed his coat around her shoulders. "What happened in there, love?" He rested a hand on her back.

She shivered uncontrollably, her teeth chattering. Shock setting in, most likely. "He took me. He . . . kept me. And a woman . . . I . . . Oh God, I couldn't help it. I had to do it."

Tracy called for backup, and as the woman leant into Damon, Tracy turned to Cowdell.

"Look after her, will you? You're a good bloke, right?" she said, jerking her head at the blood-drenched twig in Damon's arms.

Simon nodded. "I'll get her some blankets in a minute."

Tracy said to the woman, "Did what? What did you have to do?"

"I stabbed him."

Tracy swallowed. "Go with Simon, okay? We have to get in there, in that house you came from. Simon won't hurt you, I promise."

Damon led her to Cowdell, and once they were inside, Cowdell assuring her she'd be fine and he'd make her a cup of tea and a sandwich, Tracy and Damon went to the car to take their belts and vests out of the boot, strapping them on then picking up a Taser each.

"What the fuck are we going to find in there?" she asked, glancing at the house and securing her Taser in the belt beside her baton.

“I don’t know,” he said, “but I hope to fuck Chrissy Ordsall is all right.”

Chrissy Ordsall. The surly nurse who’d been in charge the night Irene Roberts had gone missing. What the fuck was a killer doing in *her* house?

CHAPTER TWENTY-FOUR

He stares at the ceiling and wonders if he'll die here, bleeding out, or whether that bitch alerted someone upstairs and they'll come for him, save him, and he'll go to hospital and then prison.

What does he want? He asks himself that over and over, and he doesn't know anything much except he just needs this to stop. He's always needed it to stop. If he'd managed to kill the one who'd just stabbed him, he could have added her to his collection, and no one would have been any the wiser. He could've gone back to his happier self, his happier life, and continued with his relatively new existence, out of these clothes.

He never wants to wear the trousers, the shirt, and the taupe tie again.

If he's saved, he never will.

He rolls onto his side on the floor and looks at Dirty Girl. Musters enough strength to rip a hole in the bag over her head then tugs on it to open it enough to see the windows to her soul. He hauls her onto her side, too, and she stares back at him, her eyes still clear. If another two hours pass without anyone finding them, those irises of hers will be cloudy, and her spirit will definitely be gone.

He doesn't like the colour of her eyes. They're not quite the same shade as Mrs Roberts'.

He feels around and brushes his fingertips over one of the glass eyeballs that fell off the table when that stupid cow emptied the bag earlier. Ah, there's a second one. He sets them between him and Dirty Girl, then reaches out, wincing at the sharp pain the movement produces. His side throbs where the scissors went into him, once, twice, three times, and a fourth for good measure, the bitch grunting every time she'd pushed them in. His shirt lifts a little, heavy with blood, and a slurping sound lets him know the material is soaked.

He won't last long.

Digging a finger and thumb into Dirty Girl's eye socket, he grips and yanks, gritting his teeth against the agony searing through him. He wrestles with the task for a minute or two, then lets her eyeball dangle over her cheek.

He pushes a glass one inside the gaping hole.

There, that looks better.

He's about to do the same with the other one, but footsteps clatter in the hallway above, then there's the heavy tread of boots on the stairs, and he knows his time is up. His body convulses, and he drops the second glass eyeball, unable to breathe in more air. Lungs straining, his heartbeat thudding slower with each microsecond that ticks by, he closes his eyes and waits for death to come.

CHAPTER TWENTY-FIVE

After checking the house with Damon, clearing each room, Tracy stood beside him in the hallway, not daring to move. Something had scuffed, or someone had sighed raggedly, the sound coming from the basement; the door was ajar, and a light was on down there. Something stank to high heaven.

She glanced at him and raised her eyebrows: *What the fuck was that?*

He shrugged and lifted his pointer finger as if to tell her to stay put.

So, he thought he was going down first, did he?

She narrowed her eyes at him, mouthing *no*, but he ignored her and shifted backwards to the wall beside the door. How could she let him lead the way when he'd been stabbed before? No, it was her turn to suffer any injuries, thank you, and she darted to the doorway, taking the first step down before he could stop her.

Nothing except the floor was visible below — the stairs were hugged by a wall either side — so she'd be going in blind until she turned left at the bottom. Heart skittering, she ventured forward, taking the steps lightly so she didn't create too much noise. It seemed Damon was doing the same — there was barely any noise behind her, although she sensed his presence close. He rested a hand on her shoulder, giving it a squeeze, but she didn't twist to look up at him; he'd only try to persuade her to let him overtake her.

Not a fucking chance.

On she went, and with only two stairs to go, she took a deep breath, releasing it quietly. Grabbing her Taser, she pressed her back to the wall on her right then shuffled along it to the adjacent wall opposite the stairs. She glanced across into the room, her guts spasming. Three naked people stood ahead of her at the back, staring at her as though shocked she was there — their eyes bulged — and it took her a second to realise they weren't real.

Mannequins.

She switched her attention to the rest of the space. A table with blood on it, and beside it, to the right, two people on the floor . . . and more blood.

Tracy motioned to Damon, who was still on the stairs. She held her hand up and showed two fingers to indicate how many people they had to deal with. He joined her and looked across, then darted forward, dropping to his knees to check for a pulse on a man, light-brown wiry hair, moustache to match, trousers, shirt, tie, blood soaking his front. Tracy went to the woman — or she assumed it was a woman, going by the clothing. She had a plastic Morrisons bag over her head, her back to Tracy, who leant over her.

"Oh, fucking hell!" Tracy recoiled. "Damon, take a gander at her, will you?"

He stared. "What the *hell* went on here? He's dead, by the way."

Tracy stood and walked to stand behind Damon. She stared at the woman, the bag split into a small rectangular opening, just enough to expose the eyes. One of them dangled out on a phlegmy thread, and what appeared to be a fake one sat in the socket, too large for the hole, so it looked like the victim was in shock. Her other eye was intact, in place.

"What's with the eyes?" she asked.

Damon stood and glanced around. "What's with *them* more like." He jerked his head in the direction of the mannequins, then walked up to them. "Um, this skin has been sewn together . . ."

"What?" Tracy went over and inspected them. "*Real* skin?"

"Maybe. Christ Almighty . . ." Damon pulled out his phone. Dialled. "I'll ring the front desk," he said to Tracy, then, "Damon Hanks. What's the ETA on our backup?" He paused. "Okay. Send Gilbert and SOCO along, will you? Yep. A bloody mess, pardon the pun and all that." He ended the call and slid the phone away.

"Sorry, but I'm waiting outside," Tracy said. "This is too weird for me. Plus, we really should get protective clothing on now."

Damon nodded.

Tracy trudged upstairs, clammy and tainted by the scene. Out on the path, she took a deep breath. Whatever the fuck had happened down there was anyone's guess, although the woman who had come out of there earlier had stabbed the man. Who was the woman on the floor, and, if those mannequins really were covered in real human skin, who were the victims?

And where the hell was Chrissy Ordsall?

"Damon," she said as he came to stand beside her. "Ordsall?"

"I'll get on to Blooming Age. She might well have swapped shifts or something." He made the call.

Tracy walked to the car and took out the whites and gloves. She put hers on over her clothing, then went to Cowdell's door and knocked. She thought about the taxi. If it belonged to the dead man in the basement, he'd deliberately registered it to a neighbour. That indicated he'd intended to pick up victims in it — he'd known exactly what he'd been doing.

Drawn out of her thoughts by the door opening, she smiled at Cowdell. "Is she okay?" she asked.

"She's in the kitchen, eating. Hasn't said a thing." He looked Tracy up and down.

"Ah." She gestured to her white suit. "Standard procedure." She didn't want him knowing there were dead people in that house yet. "An officer will be here in a second to take over looking after . . . God, don't even know her name, do we."

The sound of tyres on the road had her turning. She left Cowdell standing there and walked towards the police car and waited for it to park. PC Newson got out, as did a female officer. Tracy hadn't met her before.

"Boss," Newson said.

"Two houses to deal with here," Tracy said. "Lady in this one behind me. Said she stabbed a man in the one down there — see the door open?"

Newson nodded. "That's Claudia Pringle with me, by the way."

"Thanks for letting me know her name," Tracy said. "No Simone with you?"

"Off sick, boss."

Claudia made her way around the front of the car and stood beside Newson.

"Claudia, you sit with the woman. She'll need someone to comfort her while we work out what's gone on here." Tracy grimaced. "Don't let her wash that blood off just yet. Once SOCO get here, I'll send someone by to deal with her. Swabs and whatever. Newson, you stand at the front door over there and sort the scene log, all right?"

He nodded and strolled off.

Tracy led Claudia up Cowdell's path. "This is Simon." She smiled. "He's been looking after the woman. Try to get her name out of her. Write *everything* down, okay? Oh, and call a doctor for her."

"Yes, ma'am."

Tracy bristled. "Boss."

Claudia raised her eyebrows. "Boss."

Claudia went inside with Cowdell. Tracy left them to it and met up with Damon.

"Any luck on Ordsall?" she asked.

"No. She isn't due into work until tomorrow night. Maybe she went out." He shrugged.

"She didn't say she lived with anyone, did she?" Tracy thought back to their conversations with Ordsall. No mention of a housemate or boyfriend.

"Didn't come up on her address when the team did searches on all the nurses either," Damon said. "No other person registered here."

"That's not unusual when you think about it. The bloke may have only just moved in. I mean, look at what's-his-face, that fella . . . Pete Hewson, Jasmine Locke's ex-partner. He was recorded as living at her house, but he wasn't. Could be the same deal here."

Damon turned his lips down. "Could be." He bobbed his head. "Gilbert and SOCO."

Tracy pointed at the crime scene house so Gilbert knew where to park. He drew up at the kerb and got out, smiling at them over the roof of his car.

"Anything juicy for me?" Gilbert asked, going to his boot and taking out his medical bag.

"Um, it's unusual to say the least," Tracy said. "Downright weird, if you ask me."

"Weird is good. Breaks the monotony." Gilbert chuckled, shut the boot, and stepped onto the path. "So what's happened from your perspective?"

Tracy explained about the woman running out and confessing to stabbing a man. "So we went in. Man in the basement, lying opposite a woman who has a bag on her head with a hole in it, just her eyes showing — three eyes."

"Pardon?" Gilbert eased his head back in disbelief.

"You heard me. Three eyes. And as for the rest . . ." Tracy sighed. "You'll see soon enough. You're going to be busy, put it that way."

"Ah, well, better than being bored, I suppose."

"Someone's needed to get swabs off the woman in the house down there," Tracy said.

"I'll get an officer on that now." Gilbert wandered away to speak to SOCO, all of them putting on protective clothing.

"They've got a task and a half in there," Damon said.

"Yep. Working well into the night and through until morning, I reckon." Tracy went to rub her forehead but remembered she had gloves on.

She didn't speak for a while, thinking about where Lisa fitted into this equation. Where was she right now? Out on the streets, working? Was she living with Ordsall — and was the taxi hers?

Bloody hell . . .

"Come on then," Gilbert called. "The dead await." He laughed and walked up the path, signed the log Newson held out, then went inside.

SOCO followed, as did Tracy and Damon, all of them signing in. Some officers split off the group and went to other rooms in the house. The rest trooped into the basement. Tracy and Damon trailed behind them and waited while a petite female took photographs.

Gilbert stood with them. "I see what you mean. Taxidermy after a fashion." He jabbed a thumb towards the mannequins. "Might have the devil of a job working out who that skin belongs to. Three different people. Good luck with that."

"Thanks," Tracy said. "We'll sodding well need it."

It took a few minutes for all the images to be snapped, then Gilbert ambled over to the bodies. "That bag was opened after she died. She suffocated. The signs are there." He pointed to his eyes. "And as for hers . . . That's a glass one, same as on the table."

Tracy hadn't noticed them before — too much else to focus on — but, yes, several eyeballs were on the table. *What the actual?* She studied the mannequins. The eyes were the same. They were dealing with one sick motherfucker.

"He's been stabbed with those scissors there." Gilbert pointed. "So I'd say he — or the woman who stabbed him — opened that bag on her head and took her eye out to replace it with a glass one. Nowt queer as folk."

"Twisted, I'd say." Tracy pursed her lips.

"That as well." Gilbert crouched. "Let's have a look at you then, shall we?" His features softened as he looked at the male victim. "Come and stand by me so you can see better, Tracy."

She did, but Damon stayed where he was, by the wall near the stairs.

Gilbert undid the man's shirt buttons. "Oh, what's this then?"

Tracy frowned.

The man's chest was wrapped in wide bandages, from beneath the armpits to halfway down his torso. Gilbert fished about in his bag and withdrew some scissors. He cut the material from the bottom up, and as it parted, breasts were revealed.

"Oh Lord!" Gilbert said.

Tracy sucked in a breath. "It's a fucking *woman*?"

CHAPTER TWENTY-SIX

Tracy moved closer. Yes, definitely a female chest. "Take off that moustache? Unless it's an unfortunate real one, that is."

Gilbert took an evidence bag out of his, laughing all the while. Then he picked up tweezers and peeled the strip of hair off, popping it into the bag. He passed it to a SOCO. "Wig?"

"Seems so."

He removed it.

Tracy blinked, her heart missing a beat. "Fuck me, Damon. Look who it is."

He stepped forward a few paces. "*Ordsall?*"

Tracy nodded. "Um, this is too odd, but at the same time, it makes sense." What *didn't* make sense was why Lisa's hair had been found on Irene Roberts' pillow. "Ordsall had access to Roberts. She covered her tracks well, I have to say. I didn't suspect her at all."

"Why is she dressed as a man, I wonder?" Gilbert passed the wig to another officer.

"God knows. The obvious reason is a disguise. But if she's the person who killed those people over there" — she pointed to the mannequins — "then sewed them up over what I assume is a body shape of sorts underneath, why did she do *that?*"

Damon coughed. He was probably having a hard time being here with five dead people. "Um, what's the woman whose hair matches You Know Who got to do with all this? How did she even get involved?"

"Your guess is as good as mine." Tracy shrugged. *Maybe she's doing a repeat of the Collier case. Helping to kill people because she knows it'll be me who finds them. She's got my attention — she's in my mind, exactly how she wants it.*

"Well, I hate to break up your little chat, but let's get down to business," Gilbert said. "He — or rather, *she* was stabbed — as you said. Four times in spaced-out places, so I'd say it rings true with a panicked attack — self-defence as it were. Now the other one . . . Suffocated with the bag, that's a given. I'll just check whether there's anything else going on with her."

Gilbert moved behind the bag-headed woman. "Pass me my snippers, would you? They're in my case, in one of the transparent pockets."

Tracy found them, passing them over.

"Thanks." Gilbert cut the yellow cable tie at her neck and held it up in the snipper's grip.

Damon fetched an evidence bag, opened it, and Gilbert dropped the tie inside. He carefully took the bag off, and Tracy held back a scream. Purple hair spilled out, and now the face was exposed, the features matched those etched in Tracy's brain, ones she'd never forget.

"Jesus Christ," Damon said. "It's *her*."

Oh, it was *her* all right, and Tracy staggered backwards, unable to stop staring, needing to make sure it *was* her, really her, and it wasn't some mirage she *wanted* to see instead.

Laughter bubbled up inside her, and she folded her lips over her teeth to stop any sound coming out. Euphoria streaked through her — it was over, it was the end of her nightmare, and she didn't need to find Lisa and kill her, because she was already dead. Ordsall had suffocated her for whatever reason, but it didn't matter anymore. Tracy didn't care how Lisa had died, or why, just that she had.

She dared to look at Damon.

He moved his attention from Lisa to Tracy. Said without saying anything at all: *We're free.*

Tracy nodded.

"Who's this then?" Gilbert asked, breaking the spell.

"Long story," Tracy said. *One I don't want to talk about right now.*

"Ah." Gilbert nodded sagely. "History there?"

"You could say that. She stabbed Damon."

"Oh, bugger me," Gilbert said.

"No, thanks." That was from Damon.

It broke the weird tension in the air, and while the men chuckled, Tracy laughed until she thought she wouldn't stop, until tears ran down her face and the blessed relief of liberty swam through her veins. Her knees went weak, and she had to concentrate to stop herself from dropping to the floor.

"Outside, I think," Damon said, guiding her towards the stairs.

SOCO stared at her, their faces expressing their thoughts: *Has she gone mental or what?*

She ascended, still laughing, though not as maniacally, and once she signed out of scene, she brushed past Newson and made her way to the car. She needed a moment to compose herself, to tell Damon how fucking happy she was that this had come to an end — this torture, this outlandish terror.

They didn't bother removing their protective clothing and sat in silence, Tracy sobering quickly, thinking of all the hassle to come. Okay, while other hassles had been solved, Lisa's death brought new ones. The Collier case might have to be looked at again, her team crawling all over parts of her life, insects scuttling into her private business, the Past, and everything that went with it.

"She's gone, Damon. We can move on now." The first truth she'd told him regarding Lisa. It felt good to say it.

"I never thought I'd be the type of person to be glad someone's dead, but God help me, I am." He turned to look at her, his eyes wet.

"Me, too." *But I was happy about my father and John being dead. Hell, I was happy I killed one of them. But it still won't fix things — Lisa being gone just means I don't have to worry about her grassing me up.* "Sounds bad, doesn't it?"

"Yes, and no one else would understand. Not unless they'd been through similar. Shit, I feel like you now."

"What do you mean?"

He smiled. "Thinking nasty things about people."

Tracy laughed again — hard. "Now you've got an insight into what it's like to be me. Joy for you, eh? Do you feel wicked?"

"No."

"Neither do I most of the time." Except recently, a compassion bone had grown right near her heart, the fucker.

Damon took his gloves off, raked a hand through his hair, and stared through the windscreen. "Sodding hell . . . I can't believe it's finished." He shook his head. "She's rotten through and through."

"Was."

"What?"

"You said *she's*. Like she's still alive. She *was* rotten."

"Christ, it'll take some getting used to, accepting she's really gone. I mean, since she did what she did to me, I've worried about her coming back. I've said that to you before, haven't I. Now she can't touch us."

"No." *Not in the sense you mean, but, like my father and John, she'll always be inside my head — and in yours.* She blew out a stream of air. "I had a thought earlier about the Collier case being nosed at again. My past . . . Well, more people at the station will undoubtedly find out he was my father now. It's one thing to have it on the news and me have the same surname, but to find out he was definitely my dad? Reckon they'll look at me differently?"

"The team don't, so why should anyone else? It's not like it's your fault he was your family. You didn't ask to be born."

"Suppose not." Her earlier elation had fizzled out, replaced now by body-numbing exhaustion. She rested her head back on the seat and longed to close her eyes. "There's still so much to find out. Why Ordsall killed Roberts, among other things. Was she the one who was out to 'get' Irene?"

"Seems likely. Why, though, I have no bloody idea."

"We'll get to the bottom of it at some point."

"Are we carrying on working tonight?" he asked.

"Don't see why we should. Nothing we can do now, except maybe visit Irene's son, let him know we've found who killed his mum." She sighed, tired to the bottom of her soul. "Ordsall might have killed Roberts, she might not, but we know the woman who stabbed you had something to do with it."

"I still think it was her who did Irene Roberts and Jasmine Locke. Will we ever find out who she is, d'you think?"

"God knows. Does it matter?" *Please say it doesn't.*

"No. So long as she's dead, I don't care."

Thank you, God . . . for once.

"I should really give Winter a bell," she said and got on with removing a glove and dialling him while Damon shut his eyes, probably thinking he'd get a decent night's sleep now without any nightmares. *I promise you, they don't go away, even when the cause of them is dead.*

Winter answered after three rings. "Tracy? What's up?"

"We found the killer," she said.

"That was quick."

"One of the nurses dressed up as a bloke." She rubbed her forehead. Why was she so intent on blaming Ordsall for this and not Lisa?

"Bloody hell! Any idea why?"

"Not yet. We've got another two bodies — Chrissy Ordsall the nurse, and an unidentified female. I say unidentified — me and Damon recognised her as the woman who stabbed him. She's the one who . . . um . . . lived with my father during his murder spree."

Winter spluttered. "Ah, so John's elusive killer has finally come a cropper."

"Seems so. Forensics will match her to the hair left on Irene Roberts' pillow, the fingerprints on the beside cabinet, and that of the DNA left in my father's house, I'm sure." She paused, then rushed on to get away from the subject of Lisa. "There are three more victims. Their skins are sewn onto some sort of body frame."

"Good Lord. So the case is far from over then."

"No. Lots of loose ends to tie up. Like who the unidentified woman really is, who the other three are — Ordsall, or we assume it's her, made them look like mannequins."

"This is like something out of a horror show." Winter cleared his throat. "I suggest you get off home and start afresh in the morning. I assume Gilbert's there?"

"Yes."

"Then let him deal with the bodies. Your job now is to find out who those poor people are and inform their families." *One family member has already been informed . . . me.* "Yes. Plenty of digging to do. We can't knock off just yet. We need to go and see Irene's son. I can't go home with the killer caught, knowing he's still worrying."

"You're a good sort, Tracy."

I'm bloody well not, I assure you.

"Thanks. Well, goodnight," she said. "See you tomorrow."

"You will. Thanks for closing this so fast. I knew it was the right decision bringing you in to head the squad."

"Flattery will get you everywhere. Night, sir."

"Tarra."

She swiped her mobile screen then turned to Damon, shoving the phone in her pocket. "Can you remember where Mr Roberts lives?"

He opened his eyes and dug out his notebook, looked it up, and plugged the address in the satnav. "Home after we've been to him, or shall we nip to a restaurant and eat out, celebrate?"

"Eating out it is. I'm bloody starving, and we deserve this."

Do we ever.

Tracy started the engine, and as she was about to drive away, Gilbert caught her attention. He was speaking to Newson at the door and glanced in her direction.

She got out of the car and called from the pavement, "Everything all right?"

"Thank goodness you haven't left yet," Gilbert said. "There's something you need to see. SOCO found a few bits and bobs."

"Fucking hell . . ." she muttered then poked her head inside the car. "The restaurant will have to wait a bit longer. Come on."

Tracy and Damon trudged back into the house, and a SOCO beckoned her into the living room.

"What have you got for me?" Tracy asked.

The officer pointed to the coffee table. Picture albums were spread out on top. "Found them in that cabinet there," he said. "As well as a birth certificate for a female — a Christine Ordsall — there's a driver's licence for a Chris Ordsall, but with a photo of a man on it. Now, we all know there are dodgy licences about, so that's no surprise, but why have two? What I mean is, there's a licence for a Christine Ordsall found in her handbag, but with the picture of a woman on it."

Tracy, thankful she still had her whites on, grabbed a spare glove the SOCO held out, put it on, then picked up the first album. She turned the pages and studied the photos. From a baby to around four years old, the child was a girl, then they switched to the girl wearing boy's clothing. As the albums progressed through the years, it continued to be a boy.

"Dual personality?" Tracy said, more to herself than Damon or the SOCO.

"But her mother would have to have allowed her to dress this way" — Damon hovered a finger over an image of a lad — "and not being funny, back then, it wasn't looked upon kindly to want to change your identity as a child, or even an adult. It's only really been accepted lately."

"So Chrissy's mother forced her to be a boy? If so, why did she do that after age four or so?"

"Something we need to find out."

"You're telling me. This is such a bloody weird case." She placed the album down then crouched to inspect the male licence. "You can see it's her if you look closely. Same eyes."

"I'd say it was her brother, but I know from the checks the team did on the nurses, Ordsall was an only child. Her mother is deceased."

"Oh fuck . . ." Tracy's guts knotted.

"What?" Damon frowned.

Tracy put the licence down and swiped up one of the albums. She flicked to a certain page. "See her?" She jabbed a finger at a woman beside the boy.

"Yes . . ."

"Remind you of anyone?" She cocked her head.

"No . . ."

"Downstairs? Mannequin?"

"Jesus Christ!" Damon blinked several times.

"I think we'll find out one of them is Ordsall's mother."

Damon blew out a long breath. "What the hell?"

"Indeed." She smiled at the SOCO. "We'll be off now. I gather this evidence will be at the station by the morning?"

"Yes," he said.

"Brilliant. Thanks."

She headed back outside, and once at the car, she remembered the woman in Cowdell's house. Taking off her whites and slinging them into the car, she waited for Damon to do the same, then said, "We need to arrest that poor woman in there." She jerked her thumb behind her.

"Shit."

"Yep, shit. We'll do that, call another officer out to take Newson's place at Ordsall's door, and leave Newson and Pringle to take her in and book her. We'll interview her in the morning. She deserves a night's sleep. Got to be self-defence, surely."

"I'd have thought so, but who knows what the courts will decide." Damon shrugged. "Let's get it over with, then go and see Mr Roberts."

* * *

Frankie Roberts collapsed upon hearing the news his mother's killer had been found. Tracy looked away from the sight of him sobbing on his grey living room carpet. Damon glanced at her, and she knew what he was thinking. While this man's world had been ripped apart, theirs had been pasted back together. They had no right to feel elation in the face of such grief.

Mr Roberts' wife crouched beside him, stroking his back and wailing in between telling him it would be okay, that at least the killer had been caught, that even though his mum was gone, there was some kind of justice in that her murderer would be put in prison.

Oh God . . .

"But it was a *nurse*," Mr Roberts wrenched out, his voice deep, ravaged by despair. "Someone we trusted." Up he got then, as though some force had propelled him to his feet. He paced, and it seemed anger was replacing the upset. "I spoke to her the morning Mum went missing, that Ordsall. She was nothing but kind to me. You would never know it was her. Fucking *bitch*." He spat the last word out. "Okay, Mum was being awkward in her last couple of days, but is that really a reason to kill her?"

"No," Tracy said. "We've yet to find out what her reasoning was."

"Well, when you interview her, make sure she tells you," he said. "I want to know exactly why she thought it was okay to take my mum away from us."

Tracy looked at Damon — *should we tell him Ordsall's dead?* He nodded.

She took a deep breath. "Unfortunately, Miss Ordsall is dead."

"What?" Mr Roberts whipped his head to face her, his cheeks touched by the brush of fury.

"We arrived at the scene to find someone had stabbed her. There are other things to do with this case that we have yet to work out. It seems your mother wasn't the first victim." She wouldn't ordinarily give out this kind of information yet, but it was bound to hit the news quickly, so she'd rather these two heard it from her first. "Why she did what she did, we don't know, but we will."

"She killed someone else?" Polly Roberts asked, her mouth quivering.

"Four others and Irene, and also a kidnap victim is in the scenario. I'm terribly sorry, but we have no other information about Miss Ordsall at the moment." *None I'm prepared to tell you, anyway.*

Tracy and Damon stayed a while longer, then a child cried upstairs, and Polly rushed up to see to them.

"Do you feel you need Julie, the family liaison officer back?" Tracy asked Frankie. "We can arrange that for you if you think it will help."

"No." He shook his head. "I just want to be left alone. There's a funeral to sort out once we can finally have Mum's body moved from the hospital, and then there's trying to live without her." He sniffed. Tears fell again. "I don't think I can do it."

Thankfully, Polly returned, so Tracy took the chance to leave. After "I'm sorry for your loss" and "Goodbye", Tracy and Damon got in the car.

"Still feel like going out to a restaurant after that?" she asked.

"No."

"Me neither. Takeaway it is then."

CHAPTER TWENTY-SEVEN

Tracy's next appointment with Barrows wasn't in the evening like before. Barrows had rung to offer a morning session — something about one of her more anxious clients needing to see her in Tracy's slot — and Tracy had agreed so long as it was before work. She thought of Irene and wished the woman had seen a therapist herself so her life hadn't been riddled with insecurities, rendering her housebound, unable to enjoy being alive.

Why Irene had died would come to light eventually. Or maybe it wouldn't.

Seven in the bloody morning wasn't an ideal time to be spilling your guts to your therapist, but if that was all that was on offer, she'd take it.

How times have changed. At one time I wouldn't have entertained seeing a therapist again at all.

She waited outside Barrows' door for a moment to gather her courage then knocked. Although Barrows was easy to get along with, a piece of piss to open herself up to, it was different now. Lisa was dead, so the dynamics had changed. Tracy's perspective had changed. While she was on edge waiting for the forensics to come back on Lisa's DNA matching the other evidence from the Collier case, plus her hair on

Irene's pillow, it wasn't like she didn't know it would be a positive match, but it was still prickling her nerves. Would she tell Barrows about it?

No. It's an active case.

For the next hour, Tracy would talk about everything but Lisa.

"Come in!"

Tracy entered, pleased to see Barrows' smiling face.

"How are you?" Barrows asked, walking over to the sofa with two cups of coffee.

Tracy closed the door. "Great!"

Barrows looked at her from beneath lowered lashes. "Really? Or are you just saying that?"

Tracy sat and accepted a cup. "Really. Things have panned out since I last saw you."

"To do with what you won't talk to me about?" Barrows settled on the sofa.

"Yes, but it's gone, the problem." *Or most of it has.* "And I can move on now, so can Damon."

"So with the problem gone, are you going to concentrate on Bitchy Tracy, as you called her in our last session? I mean, will we be working to get rid of her, too?"

"Yes." A pause. "But not completely. I wouldn't be me without a bit of acidity."

"Just control her then? Learn when to say things and when not to?"

"And to think appropriate things. That's my main issue. I judge too much. I pick up on things that really shouldn't be important, but for some reason, they are." She sipped some coffee. Not as nice as Winter's, but it would do.

"Do you think you judge others because inside, you're feeling you don't measure up, so if you poke at them, it makes you forget your own downfalls?"

Tracy thought about that for a moment. "It might be. Explain more."

"Well, if you're picking someone else apart, you're not looking at yourself, are you. You don't have to face who you are, what you look like, how you behave, because you're too busy facing other people's discrepancies."

"Hmm. How can I be doing that subconsciously? Surely I should know that I want to concentrate on others rather than myself."

"Maybe you don't want to look at yourself too closely because you might find even *more* things you don't like. You might find yourself lacking, and considering what you told me in our last session, you already blame yourself for far too much, so adding more to the pile . . . Do you see what I'm getting at?"

"Hmm." Her fingers around the cup burned from the coffee. "So how do I stop?"

"Mindfulness."

"Right . . ."

"I'll teach you, don't worry."

For the remainder of the hour, Barrows explained how Tracy could switch her mindset. She left the office feeling great, with a goal in mind to get rid of all the Tracys she didn't need to be anymore and just live as one or two. Or three.

Or maybe four.

* * *

Tracy laughed with her team three weeks later in the incident room. Alastair had banged his head again the night before, this time sporting an egg-sized lump. He'd admitted he'd got the injury from using the doorframe as some kind of exercise equipment, giving his arms a workout by tugging himself up.

"Why don't you join a gym if you insist on doing that sort of thing?" she asked. "Your poor head will thank you for it."

"I can't afford the gym," he said.

"Then you'll just have to suffer with a sore head." Tracy smiled at his sad expression.

Her phone rang. She pulled it out of her pocket and glanced at the name on the screen: *WINTER*. Frowning, she answered. "Yes, sir?"

"In my office, please."

For some reason, her stomach somersaulted. She side-eyed the team to see if they were watching her, but everyone had turned back to their monitors and were hard at work trying to find out more about Ordsall and her childhood. She'd left school to be taught at home from an early age, so that tied in with how her mother had been able to make her dress as a boy — if that's what had happened — but everything else was blank. No doctor's records, nothing.

Barrows had suggested Ordsall had disassociated herself with her male persona, so when Chris had been killing, Chrissy had been totally unaware.

Flicking thoughts of Ordsall to the back of her mind, Tracy left the room and walked down the corridor towards Winter's office. Nervous wasn't the word. She tried to think of whether she'd done anything wrong during the case — stepped over boundaries or hadn't followed protocol — but she'd been a good girl this time and hadn't been up to any of her old antics where she encouraged Damon to hide her misdemeanours just so she could do things that weren't strictly allowed. Like messing with a body before Kathy, the pathologist at their old station, had arrived. Tracy had taken the victim's ID out of his pocket then replaced it, no one having a clue except for Damon. He'd told her he wasn't comfortable covering for her, so she'd made a conscious effort to stop expecting him to.

Working with Barrows would ensure she stopped doing many things she shouldn't do.

She knocked on Winter's door.

"Come in."

He didn't sound stern, more like he was worried.

She went inside, closed the door, and remained in front of it. If she was about to get her arse handed to her on a plate, she preferred to be standing while he did it.

"Sir?"

"You might want to sit down for this, Tracy." His expression darkened — lowered eyebrows, mouth downturned — and he pointed to the chair opposite his desk.

"Um, can I stand, please?" Her heartrate went crazy, and she fought for breath. Something was wrong here. Either she was in the shit and she had to grovel for an apology, or he was letting her go, closing the squad down.

Don't think of the worst-case scenario. Be positive.

She thanked Barrows for that line of thought.

"No," Winter said. "Sit."

She did, legs shaking. "If I've done something wrong, please just say so quickly, sir."

"No, you've not done anything."

She shuddered with relief. "So I'm here because . . . ?"

"Tracy, we have the results back from forensics about the unidentified woman."

Fuck.

She needed the toilet. To throw up or shit herself, she wasn't sure. "Okay . . ." The word had come out shaky, and she hoped he hadn't noticed.

"As you were probably expecting, the DNA matches that of the woman who lived with your father and the hair on the care home pillow."

"Right . . ." Her pulse fluttered in her neck, and she imagined it ballooned so Winter could see it.

"As you're involved, it's best you don't deal with anything relating to the woman or the Collier case, so there's a couple of detectives from the city dealing with this. Considering the unidentified woman is still on their books as well as ours, I said it was fine for them to go ahead and try to find out who she is."

"Sensible. I'd rather not have anything to do with her or what happened back then. I'm in therapy at the moment, at my own expense, to work through the Past, so being involved would be detrimental to what my therapist is trying to achieve with me."

"Exactly."

"So . . . ?"

"The lead DI decided to compare the woman's DNA with your father's."

Shit. Shitshitshit.

"Why?"

"Just to rule things out."

"I see. And?"

"The results point to the woman being his daughter."

I know, I know, I know . . .

"Pardon?" *Keep up the façade. Poker face. Steady hands.*

"You had a sister, Tracy."

"I-I don't understand." *I should have been an actor.*

"She's older than you. Were you aware of her existence?"

"What? Of course not." *More lies.* "I grew up an only child."

"Then we need to look into where she was for all those years."

No! Please don't do that . . .

"Christ. This is a bit much to take in," she said. "Where could she have been?"

"Rhetorical question, I take it?"

"Yes."

"We aim to find out. We also want to establish whether she was your full sister or half. If full, I'd like to know, if your mother lived with you and your father, just where they shipped your sister off to, only for her to reappear years later, giving the impression she was his wife. I've looked at the file, and your father 'married' her, as you know, although you thought he'd just married a younger woman."

Her body didn't belong to her anymore. It shook, and she couldn't stop it.

"In light of this revelation, they've decided to reopen the Collier case. Go over it in minute detail. They want to make sure it was your sister who killed John . . . and not someone else."

"Of course it was her! Who else could it be?" *Me! It's fucking me!*

"That's the question, isn't it."

The room spun. Tracy struggled to draw in air.

Compose your-fucking-self! Don't lose it now. Not when you're so close to having a proper, decent life.

She schooled her features into a Tracy she'd promised herself she'd get rid of. The bitch was back. She couldn't get through this without her.

"Fine, sir. Can I go now?"

"Do you need some time? The rest of the day off? A week?" Winter looked at her, concern pinching his features.

"No, thank you, sir. I'd rather just get on with my job. Keep myself occupied."

She walked out of the room on trembling legs, struggling to appear her usual self — whichever one of her selves that was.

As she strode down the corridor towards the incident room, Damon came out and turned as if to go down the stairs. A lump formed in her throat at the sight of his dear face, and she knew, *knew* it wasn't over.

Because she still had all her fears.

THE END

THE JOFFE BOOKS STORY

We began in 2014 when Jasper agreed to publish his mum's much-rejected romance novel and it became a bestseller.

Since then we've grown into the largest independent publisher in the UK. We're extremely proud to publish some of the very best writers in the world, including Joy Ellis, Faith Martin, Caro Ramsay, Helen Forrester, Simon Brett and Robert Goddard. Everyone at Joffe Books loves reading and we never forget that it all begins with the magic of an author telling a story.

We are proud to publish talented first-time authors, as well as established writers whose books we love introducing to a new generation of readers.

We won Trade Publisher of the Year at the Independent Publishing Awards in 2023. We have been shortlisted for Independent Publisher of the Year at the British Book Awards for the last four years, and were shortlisted for the Diversity and Inclusivity Award at the 2022 Independent Publishing Awards. In 2023 we were shortlisted for Publisher of the Year at the RNA Industry Awards.

We built this company with your help, and we love to hear from you, so please email us about absolutely anything bookish at: feedback@joffebooks.com.

If you want to receive free books every Friday and hear about all our new releases, join our mailing list: www.joffebooks.com/contact

And when you tell your friends about us, just remember: it's pronounced Joffe as in coffee or toffee!

ALSO BY EMMY ELLIS

DETECTIVE TRACY COLLIER

Book 1: GUTTED
Book 2: CRUSHED
Book 3: SKINNED

DI BETHANY SMITH

Book 1: THE COLD CALL KILLER
Book 2: THE CREEPY-CRAWLY KILLER
Book 3: THE SCREWDRIVER KILLER
Book 4: THE SCORCHED SKIN KILLER
Book 5: THE STREET PARTY KILLER
Book 6: THE CANDY CANE KILLER
Book 6.5: THE SECRET SANTA KILLER
Book 7: THE MEAT HOOK KILLER
Book 8: THE BLADE KILLER
Book 9: THE SLEDGEHAMMER KILLER

DETECTIVE CAROL WREN MYSTERIES

Book 1: SPITE YOUR FACE
Book 2: HOLD YOUR BREATH
Book 3: GUILT BURNS HOLES
Book 4: BEST SERVED COLD
Book 5: BLOOD RUNS DEEP

Printed in Great Britain
by Amazon

55974467R00108